A HERO'S HAVEN

A RESOLUTION RANCH NOVEL
(BOOK 3)

TESSA LAYNE

Shady Layne Media
www.tessalayne.com

Copyright © 2018 by Tessa Layne
Paperback Edition ISBN-13: 978-0-9991980-6-3
Print Edition
Cover Art by Razzle Dazzle Design
Published by Shady Layne Media

This is a work of fiction. Names, characters, places, and incidents are products of copious amounts of wine, long walks, and the author's overactive imagination, or are used fictitiously. Any resemblance to actual events, locales, organizations, or persons, living or dead, is entirely coincidental.

MEET THE HEROES OF RESOLUTION RANCH

Inspired by the real work of Heroes & Horses... Chances are, someone you know, someone you *love* has served in the military. And chances are, they've struggled with re-entry into civilian life. The folks of Prairie are no different. With the biggest Army base in the country, Fort Riley, located in the heart of the Flint Hills, the war has come home to Prairie.

Join me as we finally discover Travis Kincaid's story and learn how he copes in the aftermath of a mission gone wrong. Meet Sterling, who never expected to return to Prairie after he left for West Point. Fall in love with Cash as he learns to trust himself again. Laugh with Jason and Braden as they meet and fall in love with the sassy ladies of Prairie. Same Flint Hills setting, same cast of friendly, funny, and heartwarming characters, same twists and surprises that will keep you up all night turning the pages.

A HERO'S HONOR – Travis Kincaid & Elaine Ryder
  (On Sale Now)
A HERO'S HEART – Sterling Walker & Emma Sinclaire
  (On Sale Now)
A HERO'S HAVEN – Cash Aiken & Kaycee Starr
  (On Sale Now)
A HERO'S HOME – Jason Case & Millie Prescott
  (Coming June 2018)
A HERO'S HOPE – Braden McCall & Luci Cruz
  (Coming 2018)

WELCOME TO PRAIRIE!

Where the cowboys are sexy as sin, the women are smart and sassy, and everyone gets their Happily Ever After!

Prairie is a fictional small town in the heart of the Flint Hills, Kansas – the original Wild West. Here, you'll meet the Sinclaire family, descended from French fur-trappers and residents of the area since the 1850s. You'll also meet the Hansens and the Graces, who've been ranching in the Flint Hills since right before the Civil War.

You'll also meet the heroes of Resolution Ranch, the men and women who've put their bodies on the line serving our country at home and abroad.

Prairie embodies the best of western small town life. It's a community where family, kindness, and respect are treasured. Where people pull together in times of trial, and yes… where the Cowboy Code of Honor is alive and well.

Every novel is a stand-alone book where the characters get their HEA, but you'll get to know a cast of secondary characters along the way.

Get on the waiting list for Prairie Devil and the rest of the Cowboys of the Flint Hills
tessalayne.com/newsletter

Additional books in the series:

COMING APRIL 24, 2018 – PRAIRIE DEVIL

Will this Bad-Boy Cowboy reform his wild ways for the woman who keeps him awake at night?

He's the Devil she shouldn't want

Colton Kincaid has a chip on his shoulder. Thrown out of the house when he was seventeen by his brother, Travis, he scrapped his way to the top of the rodeo circuit riding broncs, and never looked back. Until a chance encounter with hometown good girl Lydia Grace leaves him questioning everything and wanting a shot at redemption.

She's the Angel he can never have

All Lydia Grace needs is one break. After having her concepts stolen by a famous shoe designer, she returns home to Prairie to start a boot company on her own. But when her break comes in the form of Colton Kincaid, Prairie's homegrown bad boy and rodeo star, she wonders if she's gotten more than she's bargained for.

They say be careful what you wish for
To get her boot company off the ground, Lydia makes Colton an offer too good to refuse, but he ups the ante. Will the bargain she strikes bring her everything she's dreamed of and more, or did she just make a deal with the devil?

CHAPTER 1

FOR THE THIRD time that morning, Cash Aiken's hands began to shake, and not from the bitter cold. He scanned the hills, barren but for a scattering of trees, looking for any signs of movement, then shook off the feeling of dread constricting his breathing. This wasn't Afghanistan. He was in the Flint Hills, where the buffalo roamed and the deer and the antelope played and all that jazz. Freezing his ass off on a six-hundred-fifty-mile trek along the Santa Fe trail. In January. On a newly gentled mustang he'd only met and learned to ride a month ago. Happy Fucking New Year.

Travis Kincaid, the reason he was on this crazy trek, trotted up beside him. "We're gonna stop on the other side of this rise for lunch. You okay with that?"

Keeping his eyes glued on the horizon, Cash nodded once.

Travis spurred his horse ahead and called out over his shoulder. "Only another twenty minutes. We can do it."

Cash shuddered and inhaled deeply, searching for calm. It was only a sense of loyalty to Travis and the slain members of his unit that kept his ass in the saddle. He'd made promises and to date, he'd done a piss poor job of keeping them. But Travis was the kind of leader you followed into the brink. The kind of man who kept everyone focused on the mission and getting everyone out safely, even when that mission went

FUBAR.

An icy blast of wind pummeled him and he flinched as a tree branch snapped in the distance, clattering to the ground. Cash lifted his gaze to Sterling Walker, who rode maybe a dozen yards ahead. The guy seemed perfectly at ease on a horse. At peace with his surroundings. Why the fuck couldn't he be like that? What kind of a man had he turned into, that he jumped at the slightest noise? He spurred his mount, Samson, into a trot and moved to catch up with Sterling. The irony that the weakest link had been assigned the strongest horse, wasn't lost on him. How the mighty fall.

Sterling gazed at him steadily as he pulled alongside. "You okay, man? You look a little green around the gills."

"It'll pass," Cash answered gruffly. "Always does." With the help of medication. But he didn't know Sterling well enough to admit that. And it didn't matter anyway since Travis had trashed his stash of pills before bringing him to Resolution Ranch. Company helped. Gave him something to focus on besides the rising panic.

"You should take a walk when we break for lunch," Sterling suggested. "Work your muscles differently so you're not as sore in the morning."

"Thanks." Cash scrubbed a hand over his beard, nodding. He hadn't shaved since... his little problem with loud noises had nearly cost a pretty lady her life. He shuddered, pushing the memory back down into the dark recesses of his mind. That part of his life was over. He'd washed out. No security or black-ops team would ever look at him again. Not after what happened last summer. The best he could hope for was to piece himself back together with a wing and a prayer. And the occasional shot of whiskey until such time as he found his mojo. God help him, he *had* to find it. He couldn't go on living like this. A shell of a man. Barely even existing.

Relief flooded through him as they pulled to a stop. By the time he'd watered and tended to Samson, his hands started to shake again. Grabbing Samson's favorite nubby groomer out of his pack, he slipped his hand through the loop and began to work his way down the horse's body. Lately, it had been the only thing that eased the shaking – placing his focus entirely on Samson. But today, his mind scattered in a thousand directions. None of them good. Forcing his lungs to take in a deep pull of the icy air, Cash tried again for calm. "How'm I gonna do this, buddy?" He murmured to the horse. "It's only day one."

"Makes BUD/S look easy, doesn't it?"

Of course Travis would materialize out of nowhere. The man gave new meaning to the word stealth. Cash nodded, throat suddenly hot and tight. "I'm not sure I can do this," he mumbled, threading his fingers through Samson's mane.

Travis clapped a hand on his shoulder. "Eyes up, Cash."

Heat flaming his chest, he met Travis's sure, steady gaze. The man was unflappable. He'd always been the coolest head on the team.

"You can, and you will. I'm not leaving anyone behind. And we'll go as slow as you need, if that's what you need."

"But–"

Travis raised a hand, shaking his head. "No one's quitting. We're in this together. Minute by minute, until the minutes make an hour."

"And the hours make a day," Cash finished, recalling one of the mantras they'd come up with during BUD/S to keep one another from ringing the bell.

"Exactly. No quitting."

Cash squeezed Samson's dark main. As hard as he

squeezed, his chest squeezed harder, cutting off his air. "What if... what if I–" the words stuck in his throat.

"What if you what? Fuck up? You already did that and you're still here. Fall apart? Near as I can tell, you were doing that when I found you, a breath away from alcohol poisoning. And you're still here. So what is it? What's the big terrifying thing that has you forgetting your training and letting fear have the upper hand?"

Anger ripped through him, white hot. "Fuck you, asshole." What did he know about crippling panic attacks or not being able to breathe in a crowd? Travis had retired and jumped right into law enforcement.

Travis laughed harshly. "For telling you what you already know? Have it your way. I will tie your sorry ass to Samson and drag you all the way to Santa Fe if I have to. No. One. Gets. Left. Behind."

"I should," Cash whispered, hiding his face in Samson's mane.

Travis yanked on his shoulder and spun him around, eyes blazing. "I oughtta punch your lights out for a bullshit comment like that. You think you're the only one? You think you're some kind of special unicorn that deserves treatment with kid gloves? Fuck that, asshole. Sterling might be more comfortable with his ass in the saddle than you are, but he's one of us. Did you take a close look at him? He buried a buddy just a few weeks ago. You're afraid of falling apart? Of not coming out the other side? You're the one who decides if you make it. You wanna live? You want another shot at making something of yourself? Then you decide. You get back on that horse, and you ride. And when you get off that horse, you put one foot in front of the other and you keep on walking. The ambush? Doesn't determine who you are. Your fuck-up with that country star? Doesn't determine who you are. Only you determine who you are, Cash. Only you." Travis jammed his hands deep in his Carhartt. "Lunch is ready at the fire. Join us. Or not." His eyes grew flinty, piercing Cash right to his soul. "You decide. And for the sake of Hamm and Jonas and Simms, I hope you choose right." Giving him a final look that conveyed so much more than anger, Travis turned and headed for the fire.

Cash tossed the groomer to the ground, watching it bounce away from the sack, and stared up at the gray sky, searching for answers to impossible questions among the snowflakes slowly spinning down. It was only lunch on the first day of their journey. How in the hell was he going to make it to Santa Fe?

CHAPTER 2

KATE MONTGOMERY BIT back a sigh as her mother swept into the living room, looking every bit the opera diva, followed closely by Franco DiAngelo, her booking agent. And, Kate strongly suspected, her mother's lover. "Happy New Year, darling."

Kate raised her cheek to accept her mother's air kiss, nose wrinkling at the scent of her powdery perfume.

Helene Montgomery narrowed her gaze. "How late did you stay up? You have bags this morning." She clucked her tongue. "You know how sleep deprivation affects the vocal folds."

Kate grimaced. *It was New Year's Eve, mom.* But like a good patient, she held her tongue and instead, gave her mother a smile that felt more like a grimace. She refused to acknowledge Franco. Why was he even here? There were no concerts in her future.

Across the room, her fiddle player and best friend, Cheyenne, cleared her throat. "We weren't up *that* late, Mrs. Montgomery. Scout's honor. Kate and I both turned in right after midnight."

Helene swung around. "*Nothing* is more important than Kaycee's recovery. And as a trusted band member, I think you'd keep in mind that her recovery impacts your livelihood too."

Cheyenne arched a brow and lifted a shoulder. "Sorry to disappoint you, Mrs. Montgomery, but I was in demand before I met *Kate*, and I'll keep playing gigs with or without her. I think you have more to lose from *Kate's* prolonged recovery than me."

Kate gave a silent cheer, heart swelling at the way Cheyenne never backed down from a fight with Helene. And Helene Montgomery was a force of nature. Iron-willed and unstoppable once she decided she wanted something. It had been that iron will which had propelled the name Kaycee Starr to the top of the country charts years ago, and where it still sat, months after she'd gone to ground to recover from vocal surgery away from the prying eyes of the press.

Helene stiffened. "I have nothing but Kaycee's best interest at heart."

Cheyenne crossed her arms, eyes flashing. "Is that so?" She cocked her chin at Franco who lingered at the edge of the room, clearly uncomfortable. "How much money did you and Frankie here lose from the last round of canceled concerts? Five, ten million?"

The accusation spurred Franco to action. "I think it's time you left, Cheyenne. We have a spring tour to plan."

She ignored him, prodding Helene. "All I've heard for months is talk about Kaycee's return to the stage. No concern about your daughter? What about *Kate's* best interests, Mrs. Montgomery? How do you think it feels having to hide from the press permanently camped at the edge of the drive? Having to sneak out of the house in disguise to get to the doctor? Hardly speaking, *for months?* Not to mention the gossip? Everyone in the biz knows something's up."

They had for months. And they circled like sharks at the first hint of blood. First it had been the increased security presence when an obsessed fan had crossed the line. Then it had been her sudden disappearance, followed by a string of canceled tours. But her mother had insisted bad press was better than no press, and that her name in the tabloids was responsible for her continued success while she convalesced.

Helene started toward Cheyenne. "Now look here, young lady–"

Enough. Kate slapped her hands on the coffee table, banging until both women turned with a start. "Stop," she called hoarsely.

Helene's eyes widened in shock. "Don't talk. You'll ruin your voice."

Kate would have laughed if it didn't hurt so much. Each visit to the doctor further dimmed the hope she'd clung to all these months that she'd be back to normal soon. She gesticulated wildly, letting her frustration come out in her hands.

Helene pressed her lips together, shaking her head vehemently. "You just need a few more months of vocal rest."

And then what? Months of speech therapy? Walking on eggshells, living in terror that a laugh, a cough, would put her back in the doctor's chair? How in the hell could she get through a set, let alone a concert like that? She couldn't. Grabbing her hair and shaking her head in a silent scream, she rose, running through the expansive room, not seeing the floor to ceiling windows that looked through the trees to the meadow and the pond below. Down the hall to the kitchen, the friendliest room in the lonely house, to where she'd left her notebook.

It pained her to admit that Cheyenne was right. It hit her like a kick in the gut. Her mother and Franco would never listen to her. Somewhere in her journey to stardom, her mother had ceased being a proud mama and looked at her only with dollar signs in her eyes. Pain knifed through her throat as it tightened. Kate blinked rapidly. She couldn't afford to break down now. If she gave in to tears now, all the despair and worry she'd bottled up for months would spill out and she wouldn't be able to stop. And that would be bad for her voice too.

Pulling in a shaky breath, she listened to the angry voices carry down the hall. Her heart punched a hole in her chest as she wrestled with her fear. It was time. Beyond time. The months of enforced silence had given Kate more than enough time to reflect. She glanced at her left wrist where the temporary tattoo she'd put on last night with Cheyenne peeked up at her in bold script. *Brave.*

What she planned to do might hurt, but she could be brave.

Grabbing her notebook and a sharpie, Kate marched back to where the noise had escalated into shouting. She paused at the door, taking in the scene. Cheyenne vibrated with righteous indignation as she stood toe to toe with Franco. Helene's composure had slipped, her face twisted into a condescending sneer.

The corner of Kate's mouth tipped up. Cheyenne was scrappy. She wasn't afraid of anyone. Or anything, as far as Kate could tell. Just for once, she wanted that. Wanted just a fraction of Cheyenne's fearlessness. Wanted the courage to say what she really thought, not what everyone expected. Kaycee Starr always said the right thing. Charmed the pants off the press. Smiled benignly at the creepy advances from men twice her age who only saw her as a decoration for their arm. Listened to her mother and did what she was told. Kate Montgomery not so much. Kate Montgomery wanted to kick ass and take names. Kate Montgomery wouldn't let people treat her like some object to be used or manipulated. She glanced at her wrist again. *Brave.* Kate Montgomery was brave, and if she didn't feel brave, she could fake it 'til she made it.

Bringing her fingers to her lips, she let out a deafening whistle. *Ouch.* Her throat cried in protest, but it had done the trick. Three sets of eyes turned to stare at her. She scribbled on her notepad and held it up. Helene's eyes grew wide. "Don't be melodramatic, Kaycee darling," she snapped.

I'm Kate. I'm Kate. I'm Kate. She shook her head and glared at her mother, then wrote on the flip side. *OUT.*

"I don't think you can do that," Franco sputtered.

"Actually, she can," Cheyenne answered. "And she just did, so now would be a good time to go."

Helene's mouth tightened, making her look more like a prune than a concerned parent. "You don't mean that, Kaycee. You're tired. You used to do this when you were overly tired as teenager."

And I was too afraid to stand on my own two feet. Kate flipped the page back, underlining the words and adding a few exclamation points for emphasis. *YOU'RE FIRED!!!!!!!!* She pointed to the front entry, flicking her wrist.

Her mother's gaze sharpened, turning to steel. "You don't know what you're doing. There will be consequences for this."

There always are. Kate stood her ground, not flinching under her mother's scrutiny, and slowly tilted her head toward the entryway. Helene stayed rooted to the floor, expression daring her to make another move. *I am brave. I am brave.* Heart racing, Kate spun and marched to the foyer, heaving the door wide, gripping the knob to disguise the shaking in her hands. After what seemed like ages, her mother and Franco followed. Franco didn't say anything, but his face was red. He was one of the most sought-after agents in country music. He'd probably never been unceremoniously dumped before. Kate shoved down a bitter laugh. First time for everything.

Her mother paused in the doorway, staring at her for a long moment. Surely she understood why this was necessary? Why it was time for her to go it alone for a while? Helene had been young once too. With big dreams and hopes. And yes, she'd put them aside when she discovered she was pregnant, but Kate had made sure her mother would never want for anything. She'd been a good daughter and done the right thing.

"We'll discuss this later," Helene spoke tightly and swept out the door.

CHAPTER 3

K ATE DEFLATED AT the barb in her mother's voice. Blinking back the sudden prickles in her eyes, she quietly shut the door and sank to the floor against it, hands tingling from the adrenaline flowing.

After a minute, footsteps sounded on the tile floor. "Can I make you a cup of tea?" Cheyenne asked gently.

"Sure," she whispered, pulling herself to her feet and following Cheyenne down the hall. She sank onto a stool at the long granite countertop, staring at but not seeing Cheyenne put on the hot water.

Cheyenne pulled out two mugs and squeezed the plastic bear, filling the bottoms with honey. Then she reached for a lemon and rolled it against the counter. "Well. That was exciting."

Understatement of the year. Kate pushed down a giddy laugh. She couldn't laugh. Not now. But the feeling pushed up, demanding to be let out. Her shoulders shook from holding it in.

Cheyenne smirked. "I've never seen Franco so mad he looked constipated."

Kate laughed hoarsely, trying to control the shaking. "Stop. You know it's not good for me," she said, even as more giggles bubbled up.

Cheyenne's mellower chuckle joined her. "Maybe it's just

what you need. They say laughter is the best medicine."

"Unless you're a singer." Her sides began to ache. "Singers aren't allowed to laugh."

"Wrong." Cheyenne caught her eyes and started to laugh again. "Only repressed assholes aren't allowed to laugh."

Why was that so funny? Kate gave in to another fit of giggles. Voice be damned. This felt *good.* The two women laughed until tears streamed from their eyes and the pot whistled. Kate wiped her eye. "I shouldn't have done that," she spoke quietly again, like she'd been instructed by the otolaryngologist.

Cheyenne handed her a steaming mug. "Aww hell. Who're we kidding, Kate? You're done. You won't even get hired on to wait tables at the Bluebird Café after this."

They looked at each other and dissolved into another fit of giggles. Kate laughed until her throat hurt. "Do you really think I'm done?" She asked soberly after taking a sip of the soothing liquid.

Cheyenne turned serious. "Have you tried singing?"

Kate shook her head.

"Too afraid?"

She nodded. No use keeping the truth from her. Cheyenne was no dummy.

Cheyenne peered at her over the lip of the mug. "Well… you could always adopt four cats and take up knitting."

Kate didn't want to smile, but she couldn't help it. Cheyenne had tried for years to teach her to knit, with disastrous results, finally giving up on their last tour.

"Okay. So no knitting in your future. What do you want to do?"

That was the crux of it. She had no clue. She'd been trained to do one thing from childhood, and she'd performed like a circus monkey, doing exactly what was expected of her, and taking her reward in praise and false affection. "That's just it," she wailed hoarsely. "I don't know. I don't even know who I am outside of Kaycee Starr." She buried her face in her hands. "I just want to be Kate. And go someplace where no one's ever heard of Kaycee Starr. Someplace where I can be *me*. Find *me*."

Cheyenne pulled on her hands, clasping them together. "Everyone deserves that chance, Kate. But I can tell you this. The Kate I know is strong. And brave. You just need to get more comfortable with her. And maybe now with your mom and Franco out of the way, you can do that."

Kate shook her head sadly. "But not here. How can I do that with momma hovering and the press circling like sharks? Following me everywhere in town?"

"Then we get you out of here."

"But where? Where could I go?" Someone was sure to recognize her. People who packed stadiums full of people, people who had *stalkers* didn't have the luxury of wandering around unnoticed.

Cheyenne snapped her fingers, excitement growing on her face. "I think I know just the place."

Kate cringed. "Lemme guess. You're buddies with Richard Branson and he's got a spare cottage on his island?"

Cheyenne snorted. "I know this cute little town in the Flint Hills, not far from Winfield, where I play the Walnut Valley Festival every year. It's real sweet and the milkshakes at the diner are the best. People there are friendly and down to earth."

"And what am I supposed to do there? Sing for my supper?" She coughed, bracing for the accompanying ache in her throat. "An alley cat probably sounds better than me right now."

Cheyenne shrugged. "It's ranch country, and you're one of the best horsewomen I know. At least in the circles we run in. Prairie's the kind of place that if you're good with a pitchfork, no one will bat an eyelash. Work at the diner. Muck stables. I'm sure you can find something."

"Even if I can't talk?"

"You don't need a voice to shovel horse shit."

An ice-cold tendril of fear snaked through her. She hadn't left the house without a security detail in nearly a year. Even when they drove to the doctor's, it was in an armored SUV with at least four big scary looking men. And even that hadn't been enough to protect her when the fan came after her. "What if someone recognizes me? What if–"

Cheyenne cut her off. "First, the crazed fan who nearly shot you is behind bars, and you've received no new threats." Cheyenne speared her with a look. "Have you?"

Kate shook her head. Shutting her eyes at the memory of that horrible evening.

"Second, there is *nothing* better than hiding in plain sight. The paparazzi will still think you're here."

The idea took root inside her, sparking something to life that Kate hadn't felt since the first time she'd stepped foot on the Grand Ole Opry stage as a shy fourteen-year-old. She wanted a chance to live a regular life. Have friends who liked her, not her money or her fame. Maybe even go on a date. She wanted to experience the feelings she wrote about in her ballads. To shatter in someone's arms the way the couples did in the romance novels she voraciously read night after night. "It's almost too much to hope for," she murmured.

"No one will recognize you if we dye your hair brown and you go without all that makeup your mother makes you wear.

Hell, *I* won't even recognize you."

Cheyenne was right. If she changed her look, most people wouldn't recognize her. The magazines photoshopped her within an inch of her life anyway. She silently thanked her mother. Helene had insisted she always leave the house fully made-up. "That way, you'll never be like those other celebrities always looking their worst coming out of the grocery store when the cameras are waiting," she'd said. Ironic that listening to her mother's advice all those years might actually be the thing that allowed her to start over someplace new.

"When do we leave?"

CHEYENNE WHISTLED LOW as they approached Prairie's lone stoplight mid-afternoon the next day. "I'd heard a tornado had ripped through here last spring, but *man…* "

Barricades crossed Main Street, and signs of construction were everywhere. Cheyenne pulled the car into a vacant lot with a spray-painted sign indicating parking and cut the engine. "Looks like the diner got hit. I was really looking forward to a chocolate shake too. Wanna have a look around?"

Kate shrugged and nodded, still unused to the feeling of total freedom. True to Cheyenne's word, no one recognized her with dark hair and no makeup. So far. But she still braced herself for a squeal of recognition and cameras snapping in her face. Slipping her arms into her newly purchased shearling jacket, she trailed after Cheyenne.

Partway down Main, a food truck stood with scattered picnic tables and benches spilling into a park. Cheyenne turned to her with a grin. "Jackpot," she mouthed, tilting her head at the line of cowboys waiting to place an order.

Kate suppressed a giggle. The view might be fine, but she couldn't even make small-talk. A stab of envy shot through her as she hung back while Cheyenne fearlessly approached the group and in no time had struck up a conversation. Would she ever feel that comfortable among strangers? Cheyenne waved her over. "These guys say there's a ranch outside of town looking for help. Willing to pay room and board."

She gave a small smile to Cheyenne and ducked her head, nodding.

"Cat got your tongue?" drawled one of the young men, staring at her curiously.

Kate froze. Did he recognize her? Why was he staring? She shot a panicked glance to Cheyenne.

Pity filled her eyes. "As a matter of fact, yes," Cheyenne answered crisply. "Severe laryngitis."

Shame burned in Kate's chest. How would she manage on her own? She'd relied on Cheyenne for too much for too long.

The man flashed her a sympathetic look. "Aww, that's too bad. I hope you're feeling better soon."

Kate acknowledged his kindness with a nod, then studied her toes, cheeks flaming. Maybe she should go wait in the car. Maybe leaving Nashville was the dumbest idea she'd ever had. God help her, maybe her mother was right. Her throat tightened as a sense of despair filled her chest.

Cheyenne touched her elbow. "C'mon. I got our food to go."

Keeping her eyes trained on the ground, Kate slowly followed Cheyenne back to the car. Once they'd settled inside and opened up their containers, she spoke softly. "I don't think I can do this, Chey."

"Of course you can," she mumbled, mouth full of burger.

"You don't want your momma calling the shots anymore do you?"

Kate shook her head. "Of course not."

"Then it's time to put on your big-girl panties and cowboy up, girl. We're gonna go find Resolution Ranch and I'll help you get hired, and then I'm outta here. I've got a gig in Kansas City tonight."

Kate's stomach plummeted. This shit was getting real, fast. She'd never truly been on her own. "But what if I fail?" she whispered, hands suddenly cold as ice.

"Pbbbbth," Cheyenne scoffed, sticking out her tongue. "No way. You're smart. You know horses, and you work hard. Where's that tattoo you put on yesterday?" Cheyenne reached for her wrist, flipping it up. "Are you or are you not brave?"

Kate shut her eyes, willing the tears back where they came from. She pulled in a shuddering breath. "I am."

"Are you?"

"Yes. I am," she answered with more certainty.

Cheyenne balled up her trash and tossed it in the back seat, then turned to start the car. "You are." She pulled out of the space and back onto the road. "And we're going to get you a job. A new Kate. A new life." Cheyenne's mouth pulled up as she glanced over and waggled her eyebrows. "And maybe even a cute cowboy, too."

CHAPTER 4

ASH'S HEART RATE began to slow as Travis pulled the trailer underneath the new wrought iron arch with the words *Resolution Ranch.* He'd made it.

"How do you feel, cowboy?" Travis asked as they came over the rise. A new dusting of snow cast everything in shades of white and pink in the last of the afternoon sun.

"Relieved. Proud. Glad we're home."

"Think you can consider Resolution Ranch home?"

Cash nodded. "I want to try."

"You did well out there. You learn fast. Most importantly, I think you can be a help to other vets who've struggled just like you have."

Cash barked out a laugh, running a hand over his beard. "You say that like the struggle is over, man."

Travis parked the truck and set the brake, turning to him. "I know it's not. But you made a few key breakthroughs during the trek. I know as well as you, the real struggle begins now that you're back. But you're in control. You write your story from here on out." Travis grinned at him as he exited the cab. "And you have our sorry asses looking out for you. You're family."

Warmth spread across Cash's chest. He owed his mom a call, now that he could honestly say he was pulling his life back together. She'd been a saint, and he knew she worried.

Hell, he worried. At the top of his list was spending the night truly alone. The thought of eight long hours of isolation where his brain could go haywire, pulled his gut tight. He followed Travis around to the back of the horse trailer. "Can I ask you a question?"

"Anything."

Heat raced up the back of his neck and he toed a rock in the gravel, unable to meet his friend's eyes. "I... I'm not sure I'll sleep well by myself. Can you leave the door unlocked... just in case?"

He hated asking. Hated that he couldn't predict whether or not he'd get the shakes. He should be stronger than that. He was a fucking SEAL for chrissakes. But asking for help was the first step to conquering. No SEAL ever went it alone. Travis had reminded him of that over and over during the trek. He wasn't alone, and he *could* conquer this. Find a new normal.

"You're home!" Travis's wife, Elaine called from the porch, rushing across the yard to where they'd parked.

Travis gave him a thumbs up. "Couch is yours whenever you need it." He turned and caught his wife into a hug, spinning her around and kissing her soundly. "God, I missed you, beautiful."

"Not half as much as I missed you." She beamed up at Travis. "Dax too, he's been crawling the walls today, waiting for you. I finally sent him out to help Kate." She glanced his direction. "Welcome back Cash. You look like the trek agreed with you."

Who in the hell was Kate?

Travis nuzzled Elaine. "So she's working out well?"

Elaine giggled and swatted Travis's hand. "Kate's fantastic. I couldn't have managed without her while you were gone.

I think she'll fit right in with you lot. She's been great with the horses."

Her laughter settled over Cash like a warm blanket, pulling something deep inside him. Travis was damned lucky to find a woman like that. Beautiful. Kind. Elaine had the knack for making everyone feel welcome, even when it was obvious he was intruding, like now. "I'll take care of the horses," he offered.

"I put Kate in the trailer next to yours, Cash. But don't worry, she's real quiet. You won't notice her at all." She flicked a wrist his direction, but only had eyes for Travis. "And it's the shower and a shave for you, mister. No more kisses until you've removed that scruff from your face."

"Think so?" Travis growled playfully, kissing her face and sending Elaine into a fit of giggles.

Something akin to jealousy poked at Cash's chest. Not for Elaine. She wasn't his type. He preferred someone a little leggier. A little less... wholesome. But for the first time since Miranda had Dear Johnny'd him a mere fourteen months after they'd gotten married all those years ago, something close to longing stirred inside of him.

What would it be like to have a woman look at him like that? He'd been devastated by Miranda's betrayal, and after the divorce he'd thrown himself into work, volunteering for back to back tours, pausing only for equally rigorous R&R, and then diving back into the fray. Cash shook himself. All the fresh air must be having an effect on his mind. People like him never got the girl. He'd let down every single person he loved. Even before joining the Navy. There was no one like Elaine in his future. No special someone for him. With a bitter sigh, he unlocked the trailer and greeted Samson, gently backing him out of the trailer.

"Sterling's headed into town," Travis called. "Join us for dinner? You can let Kate take care of the horses."

He'd settled into eating most of his meals with Sterling, the new foreman and a former Ranger, and he appreciated how Travis and Elaine always made sure he wasn't alone. But the way their hands were all over each other, it was clear he'd be a third wheel. They needed their privacy. Especially with a baby on the way. He shook his head. "Nah. I want to take care of Samson myself. And you two need your alone time." He waggled his eyebrows, drawing a laugh from both of them. "Thanks, anyway."

Travis grew concerned. "You gonna be okay?"

"Yep. I'll be just fine." He would be, too. If not tonight, then maybe the next night. Or the night after that. He'd made it through a six-hundred-fifty-mile trek to Santa Fe through open range, and he didn't die. There were times he even liked it. Felt peaceful, even. He could manage a night alone.

Travis looked dubious. "Door's always open. Don't hesitate."

Cash waved and turned Samson toward the barn. "You two go on. I'll finish up here." The hollow feeling returned to his chest as he glanced back at the couple. He'd never pegged Travis for the sappy love-struck type, but even at a distance, he could tell Travis was crazy about his wife. And she him.

"C'mon, pal." He patted Samson's neck. "Let's get you settled."

The barn door was partially open and Cash parted it the rest of the way, stepping into the dim warmth. The sweet smell of dried clover and hay, laced with an undercurrent of oiled leather and the sharp tang of manure settled into his bones. He cherished the solace and security of the barn. He'd learned every nook and cranny the first week he'd moved to the ranch. And on really bad nights early on, working and sleeping in the barn had been his salvation. While he welcomed the addition of a desperately needed ranch hand, the thought of an interloper in his sanctuary unsettled him.

The scrape of a shovel against the floor drew his attention. Looping Samson's lead around a post next to the tack room, he slipped down the aisle following the sound. He stopped short at the sight of a luscious heart-shaped ass bent in his direction. Of course, if the interloper looked like *that*...

Sensations Cash hadn't felt in ages stuttered to life. Legs for days? Check. Curves? If her ass was any indication, check. He couldn't care less about hair color, but the sight of the thick long brown braid peeking out from under a felt cowboy hat and hanging down the owner's shoulders launched his imagination into overdrive. Visions of winding its length around his hand and tugging, exposing a column of creamy skin danced through his head. His pulse went to the races as he watched her fluidly shovel hay into a wheelbarrow. The woman was poetry in motion. She moved with an easy grace that belied the difficulty of the task at hand. He'd shoveled hay for hours. He knew how taxing it could be on the body. *Was this Kate?*

CRACK!

What the fuck?

CrackCrackCrack

"*DUCK!*" Cash shouted as he launched himself through the air at the woman, pulling her down on top of him to break her fall, then quickly rolling them over to cover her body with his.

A muffled squeak came from beneath him.

"Quiet," he murmured into her ear, heart pounding, brain racing through a thousand scenarios of what could be going on outside. Whatever was happening, he'd protect this woman with his life. He'd failed to protect people he loved in the past, he wouldn't fail again.

Another muffled noise came from the body squirming beneath him, and his attention was suddenly drawn to soft curves and heady perfume. "Stay still," he ordered roughly, bringing his focus back to his surroundings. He couldn't focus on where the attackers were with her writhing beneath him. Not when his cock was notched perfectly between her legs. She stilled momentarily, only to renew her struggle with vigor. He strained, listening for the telltale signs of an attack, scuffles, shouts, more gunshots. But, nothing.

He lifted his head, cocking an ear in the direction of the initial noise. The woman took advantage, yanking his beard so hard tears sprang to his eyes. He swung his gaze back to the firecracker beneath him and the world tilted sideways, snatching his breath with heart-stopping ferocity.

This wasn't Kate. Oh, no. This was his worst nightmare come back to life. He opened his mouth to speak, but nothing came out. Lying beneath him, green eyes flashing fire, was the last woman he ever expected to see face to face again, Kaycee Starr.

CHAPTER 5

Six months previously...

THE MAN THEY all referred to as Bones eyed Cash critically. Bones had earned his name because the guy knew where the skeletons of every government player lived. Including, it was rumored, the President's. When he was on a roll and being a real prick, the team referred to him as The Gravedigger.

"Sir? There a problem?" Cash had aced his performance tests and was itching to get back in the field. Idle time was not his friend. A former SEAL teammate had quietly paved the way for an invitation to join STORM, the elite covert-ops and security agency that had its tentacles embedded in some of the darkest cesspools on the planet. STORM operated a private security front for the wealthiest celebrities and businessmen. It naturally placed their operatives within earshot of the most influential people in the country. And STORM was always listening.

Bones steepled his fingers, resting his chin on the point, narrowing his gaze. "You're a mixed bag, Deuce." Bones insisted everyone in the organization use a code name.

"How so?" Cash's pulse tripped. He *needed* this opportunity. Needed a gig like this to keep his focus sharp. He couldn't afford to let his edges get dull. And traditional security had bored him to death.

"You have a brilliant mind. But your assessments are inconsistent. Sometimes you apply sharp tactical maneuvers. Other times…" Bones shrugged easily. "You react."

"Isn't that the point, sir? To respond automatically?"

Bones pursed his lips. "Response without thinking often leads to mistakes. And STORM can't afford mistakes."

"You can count on me, sir."

"Can I?" Bones arched a brow.

"Absolutely. My military record is spotless. I–"

"Yes, yes." Bones waved a hand. "I've read every word in your file. You're quite the hero."

Except when he wasn't, a snaky doubt-filled voice in his head responded. Cash brushed the doubt aside. So he'd choked when he was eleven. Big deal. He'd been a kid. He'd never choked since. Not once. He'd made sure of it. "Then you'll know you can count on me in the most extreme situations, sir."

"Those aren't the situations I'm worried about, son."

"I don't follow."

"That's what concerns me. As a member of STORM, even the simplest assignments are vital. To both our reputation and our intel. If either of those are compromised, the entire organization is put at risk. I've seen more than one talented agent wash out because he *assumed*. It's the assignments that look easy which are the hardest."

"I can assure you, sir. I can handle any assignment you give me with the utmost professionalism. I won't let you down."

"Let's hope so." Bones handed him a manila envelope. "Your first assignment is inside. Report to the sit room in twenty minutes for a full briefing."

Cash gave a silent fist pump. He was in. This first assignment would be a test, but he'd pass it with flying colors. Twenty minutes later, he slipped into the sit room, nodding at the three other men present. He tossed the dossier onto the long conference table and helped himself to a water bottle before dropping into a seat. He made eye-contact with the other men. "I'm Cash."

A light-haired man with a buzz-cut eyed him sharply. "Code names only, *Deuce.*"

Cash pulled back. "How'd you–"

"Let's just say I'm Bones' eyes and ears on this assignment."

Damn. STORM didn't fool around. "Got it, *sir.*"

The man's mouth tightened. "No need for that. Just call me Ace."

Of course. "Got it, *Ace.*"

Ace acknowledged the other two men. "That's Guns, and he's Ten."

"Sniper?"

Guns smiled tightly. "Something like that."

Cash squirmed uncomfortably. Not exactly the team environment he'd expected. These guys were cold as ice. But no bother. He bet things would change once he'd proved himself. The door swung open and Bones strode in, sweeping his gaze across the table and bringing it to rest on him. "There's a plane out at the airport waiting to fly you to Nashville. When you arrive at Ms. Starr's estate, you'll relieve the local security company. Do a perimeter sweep and then no one goes in or out without photo ID that matches the list in your folder. Checkpoint one will be at the drive. Checkpoint two at the front door. All other entrances have been secured. We'll employ a two-point check system at the residence until the stalker is detained."

"Sir?" Cash raised a finger. "When do you expect him to make a move?"

Bones narrowed his gaze. "How do we know it's a man?"

"This has all the classic–"

Bones shook his head, cutting him off. "It does. But this is what I meant earlier about assuming. With that attitude you'd be more likely to let a woman slip past. Until we have definitive evidence, *everyone* is a threat."

Cash's stomach dropped like a stone and his cheeks grew hot. "Understood."

Bones looked around the room. "Any other questions?"

The other three shook their heads.

"Everyone clear about their roles?"

They all nodded.

"The opening concert is in two days at Nissan Stadium. We've pulled in local security to assist." Bones lasered in on him. "Getting back to your question, I do expect our stalker to make an appearance at the stadium. To capitalize on the chaos. Be on your guard. Assume nothing. Dismissed." Bones strode out of the room without a backward glance.

SIMPLY PUT, KAYCEE Starr stole Cash's breath. She swept into the expansive living room where they'd assembled the band members, groundskeepers, Helene Montgomery – an older, harder version of her daughter, and Kaycee's agent Franco DiAngelo. She flashed them all a smile. She was taller than he'd imagined. Maybe five-eight. But it was her heavily made-up eyes that captivated him, soft and deep green as the forest behind the trailer he'd grown up in. Made him want to reach out and pull her into the protective circle of his arms. She hadn't been sleeping. He could see it in the way her eyes pinched at the corners, the slight hint of red at the bottom of the whites. And the way her shoulders pulled tight when she glanced at the four giant men dominating the room.

"Thank you for coming," she said softly, a musical lilt to her voice. "I know this is a pain, but until–"

A woman his ID sheet listed as Cheyenne waved her off. "Whatever it takes, Kayce." She looked around the room. "Your safety comes first."

The band nodded. Helene Montgomery's mouth tightened into a flat line. Kaycee turned to Ace. "What do we need to know moving forward?"

Ace cleared his throat. "No one comes in or goes out without checking in both at the front door, and the gate. Keep your IDs with you at all times. I don't care if it's your girlfriend or the pizza man. If they're not on the list, they're not coming in, and they won't be backstage."

Kaycee's face clouded. "But we have a backstage VIP party for the fans scheduled. Radio personalities, and a photo shoot."

Ace shook his head. "Not anymore you don't."

Franco DiAngelo stood. "You're a security company, not a concert promoter. You can't tell us how to run the concert."

Ace bristled. "We've been hired to keep Ms. Starr safe. Do you want a party or do you want your talent killed?"

A collective gasp rippled through the group.

"Surely we can reach some kind of compromise," Kaycee pleaded. "My fans have waited months. I can't let them down."

Ace's brows pulled together. "Do you know these people? How do you know one of them isn't your stalker?"

Kaycee paled, mouth turning down. "I don't. But there are little girls… We can't, *I won't* let them down."

Cash's mind raced, and he pulled Ace aside, not wanting to challenge his authority in front of the group. "How long would it take to run background checks on a few families?"

"We're talking thirty, maybe forty people. That's a solid day's work for one of our people." Ace answered sternly. "I can't pull them off their current caseload for a party."

Cash glanced back at Kaycee. She chewed on a full lower lip, eyes full of determination. Something about the way she held herself struck a chord deep inside him. Like she carried far more than just the worry of a fan gone too far. "What if I ran them?"

Ace flashed him an incredulous look.

"I'm serious. What if I ran them?"

"Are you aware of how many hours it will take? We'd have to set up an encrypted IP, and somehow patch you into STORM's server."

"Not if we used cell service instead of wi-fi."

Ace glared at him. "This is outside of the parameters of our job."

Cash flashed him a cocky grin. "Sometimes the battle plan has to be adjusted on the fly. And *if* our stalker is on the list, better to flesh him out in a room where the exits are controlled."

"Better to keep him *or her* away from Ms. Starr entirely."

"Don't you think it will alert whoever's behind this that we're onto them if we don't allow a VIP reception? The radio personalities won't talk about the concert the next day, they'll talk about how the fan party was shut down. She has a point, Ace."

Ace's jaw tightened. "I don't like this, but I'll talk to Bones." He turned to Kaycee. "We've potentially come up with a solution. But I will need the names, social security numbers and license numbers of every person you've invited to your party no later than seven a.m. tomorrow."

Kaycee turned the full force of her soft green eyes on Cash, flashing him a grateful smile. Warmth tickled his chest as if he'd been in the sun a little too long. He dragged his gaze from her. It wouldn't do to get caught staring at their client his first day on the job.

The next two days rushed by in a flurry of activity. Ace had insisted he run background checks off shift, which meant long days and even longer nights. Cash stifled a yawn as he took up his position outside Kaycee's dressing room door. Kaycee'd already given six interviews that day. The STORM team had accompanied her to two radio stations and a local TV affiliate running a morning show. He'd been surprised at how she treated everyone she met with patience and kindness. Not like some of the celebrities he'd shadowed at a previous security job before he'd been invited to apply for STORM. He checked his watch and rapped a knuckle on the door. "Ms. Starr? It's time for me to escort you to the green room."

The door flew open, startling him. Not from the speed at which she answered, but from the fact that she looked like a unicorn had vomited sparkles from the crown of her white spangled cowboy hat, down the white iridescent guitar, to the tips of her rhinestone boots. It must have shown on his face, because she laughed, a warm husky sound that slid underneath his professional shell and flipped his stomach. "I look pretty funny, huh?"

He coughed, smothering a laugh. "Not even a Vegas strip club has that much glitter."

Her eyes grew round and worried. "I don't look like a stripper, do I?"

This time he couldn't cover the laugh. God, he hoped Ace wasn't watching right now. "Not remotely."

"Whew. My momma already thinks my career is scandalous. I'd hate to give her a heart attack over my costume."

She was too damned charming. Adorable. And there was something about Kaycee's soft-spoken barely-there twang that intrigued him. Made him want to listen to her talk all night. "You look… like a country star," he finished lamely. He'd nearly called her beautiful. Which wasn't right, not with the cartoonish makeup and costume. Nor was it professional, but the words had popped into his head.

She laid a hand on his arm. "Tell me your name?" she asked in that sweet husky lilt.

His name rose to his tongue, followed by a vision of Ace glowering. Was this a test? He wouldn't put it past Ace to test him, see if he'd slip. Brushing aside a wave of annoyance, he gazed into her eyes. "Deuce. The name's Deuce."

"Deuce," she said slowly, adding two syllables to the name as she drew it out. "Y'all like your card names, don'tcha? Y'all play five-card stud when you're off duty?" He swallowed, mouth going dry at the way she lingered over the word *stud*. What in the hell was happening to him?

She didn't wait for him to answer. "Well, Deuce in the fancy suit, I wanted to thank you."

In spite of the glitter, he felt himself getting pulled under by her big green eyes. "What for?"

"If it hadn't been for you, a lot of little girls and their mommas would be really upset. You went above and beyond, and I appreciate it."

Her praise went straight to his belly like a shot of whiskey. "Let's go," he answered gruffly. What else could he say? She was a client, and he'd move onto the next assignment as soon as her stalker was caught. But that knowledge didn't stop him from appreciating her gorgeous ass as she sashayed down the hall in front of him.

CHAPTER 6

ANOTHER PAINFUL YANK on his beard brought Cash crashing back to the present and the very pissed-off woman underneath him. Heart still hammering he scrambled to his feet, pulling her up alongside him. "Are you okay?" he spoke harshly, adrenaline still calling the shots, because Jesus, did she recognize him? "What are you doing here?" He slid his hands down her arms, checking for injuries, she tore herself away, stumbling back, but regaining purchase as he stepped out to catch her. The look in her eyes kept him rooted to the spot.

"I was working," she squawked hoarsely, voice not sounding anything like he remembered.

The twang was there, but where was the soft musical lilt? The gentleness?

She squatted, reaching for a notebook next to a thermos, and scratched something bold on the paper. Standing, she ripped out the paper, and thrust it toward him, giving it a shake. Her beautiful deep green eyes flashed with pain and suspicion.

Cash's stomach dropped through the floor. Did she recognize him?

He took the paper. What in the hell was going on here? Angry black words spoke volumes. *KATE. Sorry. I can't talk.*

His head snapped up as relief washed through him. The

last thing he wanted to do was explain himself to her. Not now, not when he was only just getting his shit together. He scrutinized her, looking for any signs of recognition.

None.

He'd never been so grateful for a thick beard in all his life.

He'd knocked her hat off when he'd tackled her, exposing dark glossy hair, not the sunny blonde from last summer. And it was shorter. Still long, but he remembered her hair falling nearly to her waist. He liked the shorter length. And the sturdy, plain work clothes. And her face without makeup. If a pair of terrified green eyes hadn't been burned into his memory, haunting his nightmares, he might not have recognized her. But what in the hell was Kaycee Starr doing at Resolution Ranch?

Out of a fog, his training kicked in. Shit. What was he doing, standing here wasting precious seconds when he needed to be securing the perimeter? "Stay here," he barked. "Don't move." He spun on his heel not bothering to wait for her assent, starting by verifying each stall only held horses, or was empty, then checking the tack room. Once outside, he circled the barn, looking for signs of forced entry in the fading light, of footprints, anything out of the ordinary. Nothing. What had he heard? With a sigh of defeat, he re-entered the barn.

She was waiting for him at the entrance, face set. She thrust another piece of paper at him.

The noise was a truck backfiring.

No way. It couldn't have been. It sounded just like a Kalashnikov. The same span of time between shots. He dropped his hand, shaking his head, dread pooling in his belly. It had been a Kalashnikov.

The sympathy in her expression confirmed he'd misheard.

And that he'd lost his fucking shit *again.*

He scrubbed a hand over his beard, nausea roiling through him. "I... I'm sorry," he choked out. His chest burned. He thought he'd come so far, and he hadn't even made it off square one. He stared at a piece of straw on the floor. How could he look at her ever again? "I reacted," he said, hearing Bones' voice. "I didn't mean to scare you," he whispered.

He should go tell Travis. Let him know what happened. For all the good it would do, because Travis would tell him what he already knew. That all the events that had led him to this point could be a part of his story, or *be* the story. And it was up to him to decide.

Kaycee tugged on his coat, and he dragged his gaze to hers. Wallowing in an existential crisis in front of her wouldn't change a thing. He needed to man up and take her pity or her anger, or whatever she was going to throw at him, even if it burned a hole in his stomach to do it. But he only saw empathy, and softness. His chest pulled tight. He deserved worse. He'd freaked out, for chrissakes. Tackled her.

"I'm okay," she mouthed and turned, taking the curry comb out of the bucket hanging next to the tack room door.

He remained rooted to the spot, stunned, until it registered what she was doing. No one cared for Samson. *No one.* He followed her and laid a hand over hers. "No one takes care of Samson but me," he growled softly.

She answered by rolling her eyes and continuing to brush Samson's coat.

"I don't care if it's your job. He's my horse, and I'll be taking care of him."

The look she gave him dripped with indignation, but she handed him the brush. Forcefully. Then she spun on her heel and rushed out of the barn. He laid his head on Samson's shoulder, desperately trying to bring calm to his body. But even breathing with Samson didn't calm his jumbled thoughts. Not one iota.

Was Kaycee in trouble? Did she think he was a freak? Why the fake name? He wracked his brain, trying to remember anything he might have seen in the press. But he'd pretty much tuned out everything about Kaycee after her stalker had been captured, no thanks to him. Would it help or hurt her safety to let Travis know? A tremor ran down his arm. He squeezed shut his eyes, willing his hand to stop shaking.

A noise at the door pulled his focus. She was back, and the look she gave him dared him to stop her as she led Travis's horse, Flipper, to another station by the tack room. Cash restarted his ministrations but watched her discretely. Her movements with the horse were smooth, confident. If he remembered correctly, there'd been a stable on her grounds in Nashville, but it surprised him given what he remembered about her dossier, that she behaved as if she'd been around horses her whole life. As if stable chores weren't beneath her.

She worked faster than he did, and they finished at roughly the same time. Somewhere in the process of leading the horses to their stalls, then working silently side by side to feed and water them, Cash realized his hands had stopped shaking. Calm had returned to his body. When the horses were settled, he walked down the aisle, hands full of tools to return to their rightful place, hearing her footfalls behind him. But when he stepped out of the tack room an offer to safely see Kaycee/Kate to her trailer on his lips, he was alone.

CHAPTER 7

A S SOON AS the man ducked into the tack room, Kate picked up her pace and darted outside, stumbling and catching herself on the fence. Slowly, she counted back from twenty as her racing heart slowed to normal.

Who was that man?

Kate's heart started pounding again as she revisited the scene. *He'd looked at her like he'd known her.* But he couldn't possibly know her. She didn't know any real cowboys. She certainly didn't know anyone with a military or ranching background. And she'd never even heard of Prairie, Kansas before New Year's Day. Maybe she'd met him overseas when she was touring with the USO? But how many nameless faces had she met over the last decade? Countless. He could be anyone.

Silly. If he'd recognized you, he'd have told you right off. Elaine hadn't recognized her. Neither had anyone in town the few times she'd been brave enough to venture in for groceries. She never thought she'd feel grateful for the hundreds of photoshopped pictures of her that made her look skinnier and prettier than she really was.

Kate headed for her trailer, following the fence line by moonlight and its reflected brilliance on the snow. She had the property memorized now, and pride surged through her knowing she could walk it without a flashlight. Moonlight provided an equalizing anonymity she craved. And during the months she'd been sequestered inside, she'd longed for fresh air and starlight. Her most inspired words came to her by moonlight. Gifted to her by a winged muse cloaked in stardust whispering to her heart. Breathing in the crisp night air, she let her mind wander, but instead of words entering her head, she kept seeing the man's brown eyes.

Something in his eyes when he tumbled her to the ground had pierced her to her core, and tightened her chest as she recalled it. She'd seen the same wild-eyed fear followed by soul-crushing hope in a shelter dog she'd adopted years ago. Buzz the mangy mutt had instantly melted her heart. Once the surprise of being tackled by a giant had subsided, was that the feeling that had rattled through her heart? Or had it been more? A little soul-spark of recognition like she'd written about in one of her hits?

I didn't know it then, but you had my heart the first time, the very first time…

Your soul sang to mine underneath the stars, a healing balm to my scarred heart… my scarred heart

She'd been unable to resist the pull of Buzz's sweet eyes, so he'd come home with her. The man was hurting. He wore his pain like a badge, and her heart went out to him. But you couldn't have magic like that with a perfect stranger, even if she'd written about it in a song. Nobody could. Not even her. Certainly not her. Not when the only person they saw was Kaycee Starr, larger than life in sparkles and fake eyelashes.

Kate paused at the bottom of the rise, tempted to turn back and seek out the man. Pepper him with a thousand paper questions. When was the last time she'd had a deep conversation with anyone besides Cheyenne? Cheyenne was the sister of her heart, but she longed for a soulmate. She tilted her face to the stars, searching the sky. Where was her one and only? Her love song? Was she doomed to give the world the words of love but never experience it for herself? Her eyes grew wet. How many letters had she received with wedding pictures, and notes of thanks that her songs had facilitated proposals, or been the sweetest wedding dance? She dragged a knuckle underneath her eye.

Superstardom sucked.

Loneliness sucked worse.

Pain pushed against her ribs, slicing through her with the ferocity of a starving mutt grabbing hold of a bone. She nearly buckled from the force of it. Would someone ever see *her?* Kate?

For a moment, the stranger looked at her like he was worried about *her.* Was that what she was glomming onto? Was she so desperate for something real, something tangible, that she was grasping at straws and ephemeral sensations?

Get a grip, Kate. The guy tackled you. At least this time the gunshots weren't real.

Kate shook herself sternly. The man would have taken cover even if she hadn't been there. He'd just been reacting to the noise. But still… that look in his eye. She hadn't been imagining that. *She hadn't.* With a sigh, she made her feet turn toward her trailer, sitting lonely and cold in the dark. For the first time since she'd arrived at Resolution Ranch, a wave of homesickness shot through her. Too bad repurposed FEMA trailers didn't come with fireplaces. Fires staved off the loneliness, offered companionship and hope when feelings of despair threatened to overwhelm her.

She hopped up the steps and pushed open the door, heart sinking at the reality of no fire. The door clicked shut behind her, but she didn't reach for the light. Tonight, she couldn't bear the harsh light of reality. At least enveloped in darkness she could imagine a different life. A Kate life.

Taking the two steps to the table, she reached for the matches next to the cluster of votives. They might not be a fire, but candlelight soothed her when she was wound up and brooding. After she brushed her teeth, she returned to the tiny circle of golden light, letting herself get lost in the flickering and dancing flames. She slid a glance over to the couch. The black leather case holding her prized possession called to her. Her breath caught somewhere in the back of her throat. She hadn't played it since before her surgery. Would her fingers remember the notes? Her palms itched.

"Fuck it," she whispered to the darkness. If she was moving on, cutting her losses, there was no better time than the present. She reached for the handle, gently placing the case on the floor. The snick of the latches releasing bounced off the walls. Hands trembling, she flipped the lid, heart tripping as the scent of wood and polish hit her nose. She lifted the guitar from its case reverently, greeting her old friend, her confidante. She'd poured all her teenage angst and then some into the '57 Martin given to her by her late grandmother the night before she stepped foot on the Grand Ole Opry stage for the very first time.

It had hurt too much to play it after her surgery. Had only made her cry during the months of enforced vocal rest. She'd taught herself the mandolin while she healed. Something new to keep her mind out of the panic room. It had helped, and it turned out she was a decent enough player. She smiled wryly. If she asked, Cheyenne could help her get gigs playing back-up in a band. Oh, the irony.

She perched on a chair and settled the guitar across her lap. She only flinched once when the G-chord broke the silence and echoed through the room. But then she settled into the sound like she was donning her favorite sweater, and a small part of her soul returned home.

INSISTENT RAPPING ON the door startled her awake. Kate sat bolt up, clutching her robe. She remembered lying down on the couch to think, sometime in the wee hours. She must have drifted off. The rapping started again. She opened her mouth to call out, but caught herself just in time. Yelling was seriously out of the question. A quick glance at the clock on the stove confirmed it was still early, she hadn't overslept. Had something happened? Did Elaine need emergency help with her son?

She scrambled up and stepped to the door, jerking it open. The air whooshed out of her lungs as she took in the giant of a man on her steps. Something hooked in her belly and pulled tight as she studied him. His freshly showered hair glistened in the early morning light, and she caught the scent of clean, piney soap. Her favorite. He offered her a sheepish grin, white teeth flashing underneath his dark bushy beard. His eyes were soft. Curious. Deep brown, like unsweetened cocoa flecked with gold. The kind of eyes a girl could lose herself in if she weren't very careful.

This time when he spoke, there was no harsh edge. "I wanted to apologize again for last night. I was startled and reacted badly. I'm working on it, and I didn't mean to scare you."

Her heart thudded somewhere in the vicinity of her throat.

He glanced down, rubbing a hand over his head, then back up. "I lay awake most of the night thinking about it."

Him too, huh?

"Sometime after midnight, I realized I'd never even introduced myself." He stuck out his bear paw of a hand. "I'm... Cash."

Her mystery next-door neighbor. Elaine had mentioned that she'd be living next door to Cash. So he must have returned home from the trek yesterday with the rest of the crew. Kate couldn't stop the smile she returned, nor did she want to. She slipped her hand into his, marveling at the way his warm, calloused hand encased hers. But it was the zip of electricity that shot up her arm and settled at her sternum that startled her. Her pulse raced as awareness hit every nerve ending simultaneously. Her nipples pebbled and a delicious ache sprang to life at the heart of her. Goosebumps scurried up her flesh. She couldn't have spoken even if she'd wanted to.

How long they stood simply holding hands, she had no idea. But the cold finally permeated her awareness, and she motioned him in. She turned on the coffee, pulling down a second cup from the cupboard. He completely dwarfed her surroundings. He must be six-five at least, and as wide as a linebacker. She couldn't see his muscles underneath his coat, but she bet he had them in spades. Was his chest as furry as his beard? Her heart kicked extra hard as the imagined his chest. *Whoa, girl.* What was happening to her? Had his tackle the night before knocked something loose in her brain?

He spotted the guitar, lying inside the open case and looked back at her, studying her intently. She stilled. Why was he looking at her like that? Like he could see right into her soul? "Nice guitar," he said after a long moment.

Best play it cool for now. She shrugged and gave a half-nod, turning back to the sink to vigorously wash out a cup that didn't need it in an effort to hide her flaming cheeks. She couldn't breathe, the air was too thick between them. Too full of all the things she'd say if she could talk.

The coffee pot burbled to a stop, and she pulled it out, pouring and offering Cash a steaming cup. She poured herself a matching cup and leaned a hip against the counter, studying him. He held the cup gently, as if he were afraid it would break in his hands.

Kate smacked her forehead. Where were her manners? Her mother would tan her hide if she discovered she hadn't invited her guest to sit. Flashing him a guilty smile, she motioned to the table. He eyed it dubiously. "How about the couch? I don't think I can squeeze into that tiny space."

It *was* tiny. And the vision of Cash's enormous frame squashed in the corner of the banquette made her grin. She nodded and joined him on the couch, angling her body to face him. Her knee brushed his as she sat, setting her heart racing. Heat flooded her cheeks, and she studied her coffee. Maybe Cash's eyes were closer to coffee than unsweetened cocoa.

They sipped in silence.

She snuck another glance his direction, completely at a loss for what to do next. Mistake. He was staring, and now she couldn't look away. She'd been wrong about the coffee color. His eyes were more like mahogany or maybe rosewood. She tore her eyes from his face, seeking her guitar. Damn. His eyes were the color of her guitar. A thousand butterflies took flight at the realization.

Cash cleared his throat. "So do you have laryngitis?"

There he went, looking concerned again. Like he cared. But he couldn't possibly... She nodded, and stood, walking to the table where her notebook lay. She picked up her pen and wrote.

I hurt my voice. My doctor said I shouldn't talk until my next appointment.

She handed him the paper, watching him closely as he read it. When he lifted it, his eyes were full of empathy. "I bet that's been hard."

Total understatement. She nodded.

"When's your next appointment?"

She held up two fingers.

"Days?"

She shook her head.

"Oh, weeks."

She nodded.

Cash grinned up at her. "Well then, it looks like I'm doing all the talking until then."

She grinned back, his smile infectious.

Cash drained the last of his coffee and set the cup on the floor. "Thanks for the coffee." He stood, coming toe to toe with her. Kate's brain buzzed with the scent of him. As she tilted her head to meet his eyes, her throat parched. There was more than concern in his friendly, brown eyes. There was heat, and her body answered with a thrill. He raised a hand, sliding a thumb down her cheek, barely touching her and yet managing to leave a trail of fire that sizzled through her body. She breathed in sharply, and he immediately dropped his hand, looking chagrined.

"If you need anything… Kate…" He looked funny saying her name. "I'm right next door. See you 'round?"

Before she could answer with a nod and a smile, he'd stepped out the door, moving surprisingly fast and light on his feet for a man so large.

Yeah. See you 'round, Cash.

CHAPTER 8

C ASH PRACTICALLY JOGGED away from the trailer, setting out for the main house. What had he been thinking? He'd been mesmerized by those magic green eyes, that's what. He hadn't meant to scare her. He'd been as surprised by his touch as she had. And the way she looked when she answered the door... he'd been entirely unprepared for the effect she had on him. Sweet and sexy and utterly kissable, all bundled up in her oversized terrycloth bathrobe and fuzzy socks, hair in tousled waves.

But he couldn't go there with her. Not ever. At some point, she'd put two and two together and figure out that he'd failed her once before. And he couldn't bear to see how her eyes would condemn him when the ugly truth came out. No, he'd just have to keep a tight rein on himself. Besides, he was here at the ranch to work. Ultimately to help others struggling with the same things he did. Kissing would be a distraction.

He closed his eyes as the thought of that lovely distraction settled with an ache deep in his balls. It had been so long since he'd felt any kind of affection for a woman, let alone desire. He couldn't let Kaycee awaken those long-dead places. It might be torture, but he'd survived worse.

Elaine met him on the porch of the main house. "Morning," she said brightly, looking relaxed and happy.

Cash's heart gave a lurch as he thought about what Kaycee

might look like after an obvious night of bedding.

"Sterling and Travis are out in the far north pasture pulling stumps and repairing fences. They said for you to join them."

"Great. Is there anything you need me to do here before I go?"

"Nah. Kate will help me after she exercises the other horses."

So she helped with domestic stuff too? That made no sense. If the queen of country had lost her voice and was convalescing, why work? Why not convalesce at a spa in Desert Springs, or wherever fancy people went for R&R? There must be something else going on.

"See you for supper, then." Cash turned and headed for the barn. Halfway there, he stopped in his tracks. Was there another stalker? That would explain the name change and the dark hair. Dread pooled in his stomach. If that was the case, then chances were Travis already knew, and the less he said about it, the better. Travis must be keeping that intel on a need to know status. In which case, he didn't need to know. But he'd be on his guard. He damned well wasn't going to let Kaycee down a second time.

By the time the men returned for dinner Cash had worked himself into a good place. Travis was right, sweat labor did wonders for the mind. Held the demons at bay. Today his hands hadn't shaken once.

"Join us for dinner?" Travis asked everyone.

"No thanks, my parents are expecting me," said Sterling.

Travis looked at Cash expectantly.

He'd put them off the night before, and Elaine's cooking was better than his own. They'd ask questions if he refused again. "Sure, thanks."

"Leave Samson tied up here. Kate will tend to him."

Cash shook his head. "Nope. I'll get him settled and be in." Travis didn't understand his attachment to the horse, but caring for Samson grounded him in a way nothing else did. Samson seemed to sense when he was at the breaking point. Cash couldn't explain it, but it was like the horse *knew* his struggles. As he entered the barn, he heard the scrape of the shovel at the end of the aisle. His pulse kicked up. "Kate?"

Her head popped out of a stall, and she waved, giving him an easy smile. Warmth bloomed in his chest as he turned to loop Samson's reins around a post. "Good day today?" He called out before remembering there would be no answer. "Just give me one thump for yes, two for no," he amended.

Her answering thump brought a smile to his face.

"Me, too." He began to comb Samson, working out the mud from his coat. "We were up in the far north pasture pulling stumps and fixing the fences. Did Elaine tell you we're planning to bring in Longhorns later in the year?"

Thump, thump.

"Once we get the foreman's house and the rancher's quarters built, and we raise some money, that's the plan." He liked the plan. And today had been the first time he'd seen himself staying long-term. "Sounds nice, doesn't it?"

She didn't answer right away, but then gave a quiet thump, as if somehow thinking about the future made her sad.

The words came out before he could stop them. "Does thinking about that make you sad?" A quieter thump followed a much longer pause. Giving Samson a pat, Cash walked down the aisle, stopping at the empty stall Kaycee was filling with fresh hay. "Hey," he said gently, bracing an arm on the post. Her hair fell in front of her face, like a curtain. "Look at me, Kate."

The grief in her luminous eyes punched him in the gut, and the urge to go to her overwhelmed him. Before he could stop himself, he spoke. "You look like you could use a hug."

Her eyes widened in surprise, and he instantly regretted his words. Fuck, he hadn't meant to scare her. She just looked so *alone*. But before he could backpedal, she melted into him, burying her face against his chest, shoulders shaking. He brought a hand to her hair, marveling at its softness. She was so fragile. And his own heart twisted painfully at her tears. He hated seeing her this way. "Hey now. Wanna talk about it?"

She made a funny little noise and shook her head. Poor thing. How could he ease her pain? He didn't know what else to do, so he held her close, tucked under his chin, and murmured to her the way he did when he'd first gotten to know Samson until the tears subsided. At last, she gave a little shudder and raised her head.

Kate was painfully beautiful, eyes red and puffy, cheeks shiny and wet. Moving instinctually, he wiped her tears from her cheeks with this thumbs before pulling her close again. "If you wanna talk, or write, I'm here." He couldn't offer much, but he could at least be a friend.

She tilted her face, mouthing *thank you*. The urge to kiss her shot through him with the kick of a grenade launcher. He stepped back, heart pounding painfully. No matter how sweet and kissable she seemed, kissing Kaycee was out of the question. "How about I help you finish the chores?" he asked when he found his voice again.

He'd have to content himself with her smile. Being in this sweet woman's presence would have to be enough. It was all he deserved. As they quietly worked their way through the chores, Cash's brain tumbled. The woman in front of him was the furthest thing from Kaycee Starr. Kaycee had an entourage. Big hair and an even bigger persona. Kate was astonishingly, surprisingly... human.

It surprised him too, how quickly they slipped into a daily routine, morning coffee and a shared walk to the main house, then shared chores in the evening. He half expected her to shoo him out of the barn every night, but she never did. Maybe she liked his company? He liked hers, and not just because she was quiet. He'd never been much of a talker, something his ex-wife had repeatedly harped on him for. But he relaxed around Kate in a way he never had with anyone else and found he didn't mind carrying the conversation.

"So Kate," Cash called one evening from the stall he was mucking. "You like cards?"

A thump came from the other end of the barn.

"You like poker?"

Thump, thump.

"Go Fish?"

THUMP, THUMP.

A laugh rumbled through him. "Okay, okay, I get it loud and clear. You hate Go Fish." He pushed the wheelbarrow out of the barn, dumping the contents on the manure pile, and returned, filling a cart with clean hay. Curiosity got the better of him. "So no poker or Go Fish. What's your game?"

Thump,thump,thump,thump.

"Yeah, I know, no open-ended questions from across the barn." Damn, it felt good to laugh. "Just think about it."

She stepped out of a stall, holding her hands in a heart. For a moment he forgot to breathe. Her ponytail had come loose, and little bits of hay stuck out in places. Her eyes sparkled with silent laughter. When he found his voice, it came out too gritty. "Hearts, huh? Can't play that with two people." At least not with cards. His heart was becoming dangerously involved, and he couldn't seem to avoid it, no matter how hard he tried. "Ever play rummy?"

A wicked gleam entered her eye as she gave him a mercenary smile.

Jesus, she was hot when her confidence showed. A familiar ache returned to his balls. He cleared his throat. "I take it you're familiar with the game?"

She popped her eyebrows high.

"Oh, so you're an expert, huh?"

Her look said she was all that and more. "Think you can take me?" He challenged softly, a plan forming in his head as he stepped toward her.

Her eyes lit, and she held her ground.

"That so?" He stood within reach of her, hands itching to touch her. He settled for pulling the hay from her hair. "We'll have to play sometime." He forced himself to turn around and return to his chores, but he didn't miss the flash of disappointment in her eyes when he stepped back. Did she feel it too? This pull? The urge to spend more time together?

He'd be a fool to pursue it. Nothing good would come from acting on his impulses. No matter how strongly they called to him. But still...

CHAPTER 9

I N SPITE OF his best intentions, an hour after they'd finished chores, he found himself standing in front of the freezer case at Millie's Organic Grocery. Women liked ice-cream, right? Everyone knew that. Cash's insides tensed. What if she hated ice-cream? What if he picked the wrong flavor? Shit, this was a horrible idea. He should turn around right now.

"Can I help you?" A soft voice asked.

He spun, coming face to face with a tiny, curly-haired blonde wearing an enormous name tag with the name Millie. She must own the store. "Uh, no." Aww hell, who was he kidding? His neck burned. "*Yes.* I need some ice-cream."

Millie flashed him a smile. "What do you like?"

"Anything." He couldn't even remember the last time he'd had ice-cream. He remembered walking with his mom every Saturday afternoon in summer down their old country road in the woods to the Dairy Dip at the edge of the highway. But choices had been easy then. There had only been vanilla.

His panic must have been evident on his face because Millie gave him a benevolent pat and opened the case, eyeing it critically. "I think your lady friend would appreciate Rocky Road. I call it a chocolate adventure. Predictably chocolate, but with a surprise."

Wait. What? How did she? Was he that transparent?

She flashed him a beatific smile. "Men like you don't come in for ice-cream for themselves."

"Oh." His chest grew hot, but Millie didn't seem to notice his discomfort. "I'll take the Rocky Road then."

At the checkout, he grabbed four decks of new cards.

The entire drive back to the ranch, his heart kicked hard enough to punch a hole in his chest. Was this wise? Nope. He was skating on very thin ice. But he enjoyed Kate's company. And he was *so damned tired* of the oppressive loneliness that rolled over him like an M1A1 Tank. He trudged through the darkness, letting his senses guide him, stopping when his foot reached the top step of Kate's trailer.

Sounds from strings being plucked intermittently wafted through the door. He cocked his head listening, using the opportunity to slow his breathing. This was nothing more than cards between two colleagues. Hell, he'd play with Sterling, but most nights Sterling hung with friends in town. And he'd been more than a third wheel at Travis and Elaine's, so why not? Taking a fortifying breath, he rapped gently on the door. "Kate?" he called. "It's me. Cash."

He heard the sound of a chair moving and something scraping against the floor. The door opened, light flooding out from behind her, acting like a halo. His chest squeezed tight from the loveliness of her. When she smiled, heat raced to his toes turning his insides to jelly, and his voice wavered as he lifted the frozen container. "I got tired of playing solitaire. Feel like rummy and ice-cream?"

Her answering smile shook him to his core. She motioned him in and stepped aside as he entered. Four candles flickered on the table. Her trailer was the same as his, and yet the little touches she'd added – the candles, a plaid throw on the couch, made it seem homey. Welcoming.

Pushing aside his feelings, he handed her a paper bag. "I brought new cards. Four decks enough?" His chest rumbled at the mischievous grin she shot him as she took it and the ice-cream and moved to the kitchen. "Can I help dish up?"

She shook her head as she spooned the dessert into two bowls then turned, eyeing him and the table critically. They'd already established he was too big to squeeze into the small space where the table stood. "We can sit on the floor," he offered. "You want me to put down the blanket?"

Her eyes lit at his suggestion, and his gut pulled. He shoved his response aside and grabbed the throw, spreading it on the floor and settling himself against the couch. She sat across from him and handed him a bowl filled twice as full as hers. "Do you not like the flavor?" His stomach dropped. Maybe this had been a bad idea after all.

She rolled her eyes with a sheepish smile, drawing her hands over her figure. *Oh.* "Wait. You're worried about your figure?" Really? He knew beach babes in San Diego that starved themselves, but he wouldn't have expected Kate to fall into that category. At least not the way she behaved here at the ranch.

With a sigh, she shook her head and hopped up, grabbing a notebook from the table and sitting back down to scrawl something. Her nostrils flared as she wrote furiously. Shit. Had he pissed her off? She ripped off the page and handed it to him.

I'm NOT worried about my figure. I love ice-cream. I could eat the whole tub, but you're twice my size. Did I give you too much?

"I don't usually eat sweets," he confessed, then immediately wished he hadn't as her face fell. "But this is great." She eyed him suspiciously. "And I'm glad you like ice-cream." She pointed to the paper again, eyebrows raised in question. "And no, you didn't give me too much." He'd eat the whole damned thing if it would make her smile again.

She rubbed her hands together as if to say, "Good," and began to unwrap the cards. Her hands captivated him as she worked quickly, shuffling the decks. Before she dealt the cards, she scribbled another note and passed it to him.

What are we betting?

His mind went to a thousand dirty places. He'd never played strip anything with a woman, but he wasn't opposed to starting now. His balls pulled tight at the thought of Kate slowly stripping off her sweatshirt, exposing high, perky breasts that would fit perfectly in his hand. Cash swallowed, mouth dry as sawdust. He cleared his throat. "Pennies?" he asked in a voice not his own.

She nibbled on her lower lip, face screwed up in thought. He'd like to nibble on her lower lip. She raised her eyes and Cash's breath stopped. This was a woman who knew what she wanted. Keeping her gaze fixed on him, she reached for her notepad, only dropping it to write.

He laughed out loud at her next note. *Loser does the dishes.* She handed him another note, a sly look in her eye. *For a week.* "A *week?* Game on, sweetheart." He folded the note, tossing it between them like a gauntlet. "I'll up the ante. And the laundry."

She made a scoffing noise in her throat and smirked.

"Think you can take me, huh?" he teased.

Her smirk transformed into a knowing smile as she slowly nodded.

"Talk is cheap. Deal."

Seven rounds later Cash tossed his cards on the blanket,

chagrined. "Best of three."

Kate's shoulders shook with mirth.

"You just got lucky."

Her taunting grin told a different story.

"Prove it. Best of three." Truth be told, he'd enjoyed himself. The companionable silences, the way her forehead crinkled and she tapped the dent above her top lip when she was concentrating, the banter made up of hastily scribbled notes and wild gesticulations. The little smile at the corner of her mouth that gave away the moment she was going to crush him. All of it. Cash couldn't remember the last time he'd had fun like this, and the thought of returning to his cold, dark trailer sent a spike of loneliness straight to his gut.

Her mouth quirked as she penned another note. "I think you're a glutton for punishment."

He grinned back at her. "Maybe, yeah. But maybe I have your number now."

Her eyebrows jumped, and she wrote again, flashing him the notepad. "*HOPE YOU LIKE LAUNDRY!!*"

A laugh erupted from his gut at the caps and underlines. "I'll like seeing you do mine. With military folds," he added, enjoying the picture of giving her a little taste of military inspection.

She snorted, tossing her hair over her shoulder as she dealt another round. His confidence grew as they progressed through the rounds, evenly split this time. As they neared the end of the final round, Cash kept his face carefully neutral, watching Kate like a hawk for any signs of what Kate had planned. He'd hand it to her, she played unpredictably, sometimes laying cards down early and taunting him with each additional card she added to her runs. Other times, she kept her cards close and laid them down only when she was ready to go out. But this match was his, he was one card away from winning, and this time he was going to catch her with cards in her hand. The game was close enough that whoever won this match would win the game.

Kate's hand hovered over the deck, and her eyes darted from him, to her cards, to her hand. What in the heck was she playing at? Slowly, she drew. He had her. She'd tried, but failed to keep her face neutral. Whatever card she'd drawn, it wasn't the one she needed. And she must sense that he was about to go out. Then she discarded a joker.

"What?" He exclaimed, voice rising. "You can't discard twenty-five points. No way."

Kate's eyes twinkled.

"Show me your hand." He captured her hand, pulling her forward while exposing her cards.

Her body shook with laughter as he did a mental count of the points she held. He'd have won if she'd kept the joker. He shook his head, amused, but not ready to give up without a fight, and not ready to release her hand. "Nope. Can't discard a joker."

She nodded her disagreement, not bothering to contain her glee.

"I never took you for a cheater, Kate," he growled half-heartedly. She was so damned cute, eyes bright, cheeks flushed pink with triumph. Another tug of his hand and she'd be in his lap where he could have his way with her saucy mouth.

The air between them instantly crackled, like she'd heard his thoughts over a loudspeaker. For a heart-stopping moment neither of them breathed. Kate's eyes darkened, and her tongue flicked across her lower lip. Ahh, hell. If she was anyone other than the woman he'd failed to protect, he'd take her in a hot second. Send her to heights she'd only imagined in her hottest dreams. Instead, he dropped her hand like a hot stone. People like him never got the girl. He was living proof.

Ignoring the flash of disappointment in her eyes, he grabbed their discarded ice-cream bowls and stood, stalking to the sink. The thought hit him like a bullet to the chest. He'd be washing her undergarments. For a week. Fuuuuck. He squirted too much soap on the sponge as he failed to drag his thoughts away from her unmentionables. God, she better wear only granny pants and sports bras. He'd fucking die if he had to wash lacy underthings. Heat shot up his legs, flaming his body at the thought of Kate clad only in lacy, see-through underwear. With a swallow, he placed the dishes on the counter, the space suddenly feeling too close, too hot. Fuck him for upping the ante. He must be some kind of glutton for torture.

She tapped quietly on the counter, asking for his attention.

Steeling himself, he turned, heart squeezing at the question in her eyes. "I... ah..." Unable to stop himself, he stepped close enough to feel the heat of her. Clearing his throat, he tried again. "Thanks for tonight. It was... nice." Nice? He shuddered. Visiting someone's grandma was nice. Spending an evening with Kate was so much better than nice.

Her face fell.

God, he was totally bungling this. But it was for the best. He couldn't act on any feelings that might be developing between them. Ever. Because he'd fail her and he couldn't live with himself if he did that again.

He itched to touch her, and he raised his hand, only to drop it again. "I'll be by in the morning? Have your laundry ready."

He stepped around her, forcing himself not to look back as he let himself out into the cold starry night and took himself home. Alone.

CHAPTER 10

KATE SHOOK OUT her hands, as she glanced at the clock one last time. She'd been a breath away from making the eleven-hour drive back to Nashville for her final consult, but Cheyenne had urged her to reconsider. *Better to lay low*, she'd texted. *Helene is on the warpath.*

Cheyenne was right. Returning to Nashville would only rip open a giant scab. And she didn't have the energy to deal with the suffocating presence of her mother or Franco at the moment. She'd arranged to borrow Elaine's SUV for the day to make the trip over to the Voice and Swallow center at the University of Kansas. Her doctor at home had recommended an otolaryngologist there who specialized in vocal disorders. She cringed at that label. Vocal disorders. Thinking of her voice that way sent rivers of despair through her. She desperately wanted to believe she could sing again, but the pit of dread in her stomach told her it was over. Her mother's voice echoed in her head. *This never would have happened if you'd had good technique.* She was finished.

Still…

She could hope.

Grabbing her purse, she left her trailer and made her way over the rise to the main house. But she stopped short when she reached the yard. "Cheyenne?"

Her friend hopped off the hood of a rental car and walked

over, grinning.

"I told you, you didn't need to come."

"Are you kidding? I'm not letting you do this by yourself. Besides…" She tilted her head to where Cash and Travis were working on the foreman's plot. "Can't beat the view."

As if on cue, Cash turned and waved, then dropped his shovel and joined them. "Girls day out?"

Her cheeks flamed, and she shrugged, looking down. Cash stirred up too many emotions in her lately. There were times she swore he was going to kiss her and her body would tighten in anticipation, only to be disappointed when he inevitably gave her the brush-off. As embarrassing as it might be, maybe she needed to get over herself and ask Cheyenne for dating tips. Clearly, she was doing something wrong.

Cheyenne stuck out her hand. "I'm Cheyenne."

"I'm Cash. You visiting Kate?"

"Just for the day."

"Nice. Have fun." He turned the force of his gaze to her, and her stomach flip-flopped like it did every time. "Up for another round of cards tonight?"

Her stomach did the Macarena as she nodded, body going hot everywhere.

Cheyenne tugged on her elbow. "We're going to be late. See you 'round, Cash."

Cheyenne practically dragged her to the car, but as she pulled open the passenger door, she glanced back, blood turning molten at the way Cash watched her. Giving him a wave, she ducked into the car where Cheyenne bristled with unasked questions.

"Kate…" Cheyenne asked her voice dripping with curiosity as she swung the car around and headed down the long drive.

"Wait," she said softly.

When they pulled out onto the main road, Cheyenne glanced over. "Spill."

Her face heated, and she bit her lip trying not to smile. She'd never been good at hiding her feelings.

"You've been keeping things from me, Kate," Cheyenne scolded. "And I've been jumping through hoops dealing with your mother and the paparazzi. No fair. Spill the beans."

"How are things at home?"

Cheyenne gave her a sideways stink-eye and sighed dramatically. "The paparazzi are still parked outside the gate. They chase down my car every time I leave, until they realize I'm alone. And your mom thinks she can wear me down into telling her where you're at, so she's just peachy. But enough about home. *WHO IS CASH?*"

The flush on Kate's face turned to fire.

"Holy shit, Kate. I've never seen you this red. Are you in love with this guy?"

She swallowed. She couldn't possibly be falling in love with him, could she? They hadn't even kissed. For sure, deep like. But love? "I... I-I don't know."

"Do your toes curl when you kiss him?"

She shut her eyes. Cheyenne was so much more worldly than she was. "We haven't kissed."

"*What?* Are you kidding? Girl, you need to fix that asap."

"I- I'm not sure he's interested."

"Oh, he is."

"I feel like every time we get close, like we *might* kiss, he pulls away."

"Then you just need to grab that sexy lumberjack face and lay one on him."

"I can't do that," she wailed softly, still afraid she'd strain her voice. "And I feel like I'm lying to him. Don't I need to tell him who I am?"

"Are you or are you not legitimately Kate Montgomery?"

"I am."

"So what's the problem? Isn't this about taking control of your life? About being the real you?"

"Yeah. It is."

Cheyenne tapped her fingers on the steering wheel. "Here's what you need to ask yourself – is not telling them that you're also Kaycee Starr going to hurt them?"

"Nooo… but I hate that I feel dishonest. Everyone's been so good to me."

"And isn't it nice to know their goodness has nothing to do with you being Kaycee Starr?"

Kate nodded. Yeah. It did. It meant so much to her that at Resolution Ranch, she was just another person pulling her weight and working as hard as everyone else. No judgment. No special treatment.

"You have to remember, loose lips sink ships. The more people who know you're Kaycee, the more likely it is that one of them will slip, and then the paparazzi will rain down. Is a security nightmare going to help the ranch or the veterans who live there?"

"You're right." Kate stared out the window, seeing but not really seeing the golden hills punctuated by naked trees and cedars. The closer they got to Lawrence, the slower they seemed to drive. By the time they pulled into the parking lot of the Voice and Swallow center on the KU campus, Kate vibrated with anxiety, her mouth dry as cotton.

The waiting room was cold. Or maybe it was just her. She gripped Cheyenne's hand as they walked back to the exam room. Cheyenne leaned over. "I need my hands to play. Don't break me," she whispered.

Oh.

She forced her hand open, releasing Cheyenne's. The nurse came in and gave her the numbing spray. The minutes dragged by as the hollow in her stomach grew bigger and bigger.

At last, a tall, thin man with graying hair and glasses stepped in, extending his hand. "I'm Dr. Pingree. Dr. Thompson in Nashville sent your records. How are you feeling?"

Kate shrugged. "Okay, I guess." The backs of her teeth were numb. "I've been afraid to do much."

He nodded sympathetically. "I understand. It's normal to feel that way. Let's have a look, shall we?"

He pulled the snaky contraption off the counter, wiping it down and then adding a gel to the tip where a bright light shone. "You've seen one of these before, yes?"

Kate nodded, fear fisting in her chest. She hated the laryngoscope. Hated she knew its name and that she was intimately familiar with its workings.

"Okay, let's take a look. You've been numbed, and I've added a little numbing gel to the tip to make it easier as we pass through your sinuses."

Cheyenne gave her hand a squeeze, and she blinked rapidly, quelling the fear rising through her.

"Now, just breathe easy. Keep your soft palate relaxed."

Right. Easy to do when you didn't have a plastic snake with a camera winding its way through your head. Dr. Pingree worked quickly, and in no time she was aware of the camera in the back of her throat. She fought the urge to gag. This would only last a few minutes.

"Alrighty. I see your vocal folds. I'm going to try and get a closer view. I want you to take a big breath and then say *eeee*. Ready?"

She took a big breath, bracing for the awkward sensation. There was nothing normal about a camera going down your throat. "Eeeeeeeeeeee."

"Good. Again."

She blinked rapidly, taking another breath. "Eeeeeeeeee."

"Excellent. Good job. One more deep breath."

She fought the urge to gag and did as she was told, sagging in relief when he removed the camera.

Cheyenne leaned over. "You looked like E.T."

Kate snorted. "I knew there was a reason I kept you around."

Dr. Pingree flipped on the lights. "Let's look at the pictures we captured." He clicked a few buttons on a remote and pictures of her vocal cords came up on the screen. Kate's heart sank. She'd seen enough photos since before her surgery, she knew what to look for.

"Let's look at the good news first."

Nausea roiled through her. Gearing up to take the bad news as gracefully as possible.

"Fifty-percent of your varicosities have diminished. That's good. That reduces the potential for hemorrhaging again."

Yay. She should feel positive about that. The vocal rest had helped. But not enough.

"But I'm concerned about this thickness at the incision site. You've got significant scarring where your surgeon drained the cysts. There's been no change at that site over the last three months."

"None at all?" Cheyenne asked incredulously.

Dr. Pingree shook his head, giving her a sympathetic look. "I'm sorry. We don't know why, but in a small percentage of our patients, surgery triggers permanent callousing and edema at the incision site."

Kate clutched the arms of the chair, reeling. Her body went hot and cold. She looked at Cheyenne. This was so much worse than she'd ever imagined. Her heart began to shatter into a million tiny pieces. All these months of enforced silence. Of nearly going crazy from the waiting. Of feeling like she walked on a knife edge, and the only thing keeping her from tottering over was the mantra that this was only temporary. That there was a light at the end of the tunnel.

"What exactly does this mean?" Cheyenne asked.

Dr. Pingree studied the pictures in the folder, then the ones on the screen. "Truthfully? You'll probably always be a little hoarse with this kind of damage."

"But can I sing?" Kate asked. "I have to be able to sing."

Dr. Pingree made a face. "You could... But I wouldn't advise it. The more you use your voice – even in speaking, the more you'll irritate the damage already there. If you irritate it enough, it could lead to paralysis of the vocal cords."

"But it's my livelihood."

Dr. Pingree's eyes softened. "You might want to consider a new career. I'm not saying it's out of the question, but I don't advise it. If you wanted to try, you'd need to start slowly. Light talking. No yelling. And no more than ten minutes a day of singing. If it feels okay after a few weeks, move up incrementally. But know the risks, and if it hurts, stop. Or you'll risk paralysis."

"What about more vocal rest?" She was grasping at straws. In her heart of hearts, she knew it. But she couldn't bear it.

Dr. Pingree sighed heavily. "You could try. But I think it's time to consider your quality of life, too."

"So that's it?" Cheyenne asked flatly. "There's nothing

more we can do?"

"I'm so sorry." Dr. Pingree shook his head.

"Just one question," Kate asked, hearing her mother in her head. "Did this happen because I had bad technique? Because I was a bad singer?"

Dr. Pingree rifled through the folder, reading, then shook his head. "We could talk about technique. About how the vocal folds vibrate optimally, but truthfully, most vocal damage such as yours is triggered by a single event. Coughing or sneezing, or prolonged yelling, and then exacerbated by overuse of the voice. The best technique in the world won't save a voice from fatigue. It's a muscle like any other muscle. If you overuse it and don't give it adequate recovery time, it fails."

Cheyenne looked at her and raised her eyebrows, knowing why she'd asked. Cheyenne had been there when Helene had berated her. It was cold comfort now, but Cheyenne would make sure Helene no longer brought up her singing ability.

"Thank you for your time, doctor," Kate whispered.

"I'm sorry I don't have better news. Good luck with whatever you decide to do moving forward."

Kate let Cheyenne lead her from the office and stared straight ahead as they pulled back onto the highway.

"Feel like tying one on?" Cheyenne said brightly. "I know it's only one o'clock on a Monday…"

Kate laughed bitterly, shaking her head. She would not cry. Not even in front of her best friend. She wouldn't do it, even though the ache in her chest consumed her.

She appreciated Cheyenne's attempts at conversation during the drive home, but she just… couldn't. She stared out the window, wrapped in a cloak of numbness. When Cheyenne pulled to a stop in the yard back at the ranch, she finally spoke. "Well, at least I learned to play the mandolin."

Cheyenne reached across the console, wrapping her in a hug. "Aww, hon. If that's what you want to do, I have connections."

They both let out sad laughs.

"Do you want me to stay? I can change my flight."

"I'll be fine."

"Are you sure?"

Kate shut her eyes, nodding. "Yes. Okay, *no*. But I have to learn, right?" She gave Cheyenne a weak smile. "I have to learn how to be fine with this."

"Okay. I'm only a phone call away. You tell me what you need, and I'll take care of it. Take as much time as you need."

She gave her friend a final hug. "Love you, Chey. Thanks for being here."

"Love you, too. And I mean it. Say the word."

Kate exited the car and watched as her friend turned back down the drive, then looked around. Now what? Should she slink back home to Nashville? Should she stay? She returned Cash's wave from where he and Travis were working on the foundation of the foreman's house.

Pulling her coat tighter, she trudged back to her trailer, changed into her work clothes, and walked back to the barn. She took care of her chores in a state of numbness, working from muscle memory rather than a sense of connection to the tasks at hand. When the horses had been tended to, she cleaned the tack room, cleaning and polishing everything to the point it shined. When there was nothing left to do, she inhaled slowly, letting the sweet scent of hay move through her. She could still detect the faint aroma of saddle soap on her hands. Maybe if she stood here long enough, grounding herself in her surroundings, she could hold the crushing pain at bay.

She couldn't move. The thought of sleeping in her trailer tonight was too much. The walls too confining for her grief. Grabbing a saddle blanket, she walked back down the aisle and climbed the ladder to the hayloft. She didn't care if she froze to death tonight. It was better than being closed up in her tiny trailer.

Sliding open the second story door, she welcomed the blast of cold air hitting her face. Kicking the hay into a pile, she pulled the blanket around her shoulders and settled against a stack of bales where she could look out the door, the loose hay offering a tiny buffer between her body and the wood floor. A sliver of moon hung low in the sky, cradling the darkness above it.

As she sat, the music came, and with it, the anguish she'd valiantly held at bay for months. It came crashing over her in the darkness, ripping through her body, tearing her apart like she was dinner for a starving tiger. Tears built behind her eyes. And this time, she let them come.

CHAPTER 11

CASH CROSSED THE length of his trailer in three steps. Three steps later he was back where he'd started. He peered through the window. Kate's trailer was dark. Where was she? Cheyenne had dropped her off hours ago. Had they gone out again and he hadn't noticed? Maybe they'd gone into town to go dancing at the Trading Post.

But it was a Monday night. Even he knew no one hit the Trading Post on a Monday.

He shouldn't worry. Kate was a grown woman. Twenty-four to his thirty, but old on the inside. She'd lived a fairly quiet life, considering her super-star status. Hadn't exploited the club scene the way some of her contemporaries had. Every instinct inside him screamed that something wasn't right.

The clock on the stove read eleven p.m. Even if she'd gone to the Trading Post, she should have been home by now. Grabbing his coat, and jamming on his Stetson, he stepped outside. Thirty feet tops separated their trailers. He hopped up the steps and rapped on the door. "Kate?"

Twenty-seconds. Forty. Fear gnawed at him.

"Kate?" He rapped more insistently.

Foreboding slithered ice-cold, down his spine. He tried the door, and it fell open. Immediately alert, he slipped into the space, scanning for trouble. What he wouldn't give for a pair of night-vision goggles right now. He could make out her guitar, lying on the table. She'd been here then, and must have left in a rush, because she *always* put away her guitar.

Sliding along the wall, he silently pushed open the screen to her bedroom. Empty. He didn't know whether to feel relieved or even more worried. Where in the hell was she? Just to make sure, he quietly moved to the other end of the trailer, checking the shower, although it had been clear to him her place was empty. Buildings occupied by the enemy felt... ominous. His thoughts briefly drifted back to a deserted building on the other side of the world that ended up not so deserted. Grim determination filled him. Never again.

Cash made a quick list.

Kate could be with Cheyenne. If that was the case, he'd just have to wait until she returned.

She could be on a walk. Sometimes he heard her slip out for a late-night wander, but she always returned after about thirty minutes, and tonight he'd been waiting for her far longer.

She wasn't in the main house, Travis and Elaine turned in fairly early.

He snapped his fingers. The barn. He hadn't seen her when he'd put up Samson for the night, but he hadn't been looking for her either. And lord knew how many nights he'd spent in the comforting quiet of the barn chasing sleep. Slipping back outside, he broke into a jog, not wanting to waste a second. If she wasn't in the barn, he'd alert Travis.

His feet hit the gravel and he skidded, but regained his purchase. He paused at the barn door to catch his breath, then hauled the heavy door back, sliding into stealth mode as he entered. "Kate?" he called softly. He cleared the tack room, then started with the stalls, quickly moving through the space. "Kate? You here?"

His only answer was the shuffling and chuffing of the horses. Giving Samson a scratch on the forehead, he continued his search. And then he heard it – a quiet snuffle coming from the loft. If he hadn't been alert, he'd have passed it off as a horse sound. His heart jammed up into his throat. Was she *crying?*

Scrambling up the ladder, he paused just below the ceiling, training kicking in. Someone was definitely up there. He didn't hear signs of a struggle. Only quiet sniffles. Slowly he peeped over the edge, scanning for signs of trouble, eyes coming to rest on a blanket covered body, shaking and bathed in moonlight.

Cash's heart cracked wide open as he rushed to her, protective instincts taking over. He dropped to his knees, pulling on her shoulder, rolling her off her side and lifting her up to slide in behind her so he could hold her on his lap. "Oh, hon. Talk to me. What is it? What's got you so upset?"

Kate turned her head to him, clutching his coat and letting out a wail that made his eyes wet.

Oh God, what had happened? Was it her family? Had someone died? Was *she* dying? He went cold at the thought. "It's okay. It's gonna be okay." He rocked her, letting her sob, his chest aching at the pain in her voice. "I'm right here. I'm not going anywhere." He'd endured far too many nights on his own, despairing and wrestling with demons to let anyone, especially Kate, go it alone.

He settled her more comfortably in his lap and leaned against the hay bales, talking and stroking her back until her sobs subsided to intermittent sniffs. What had broken her? If it was fixable, he'd figure out how to make it better.

By the time she raised her head, the moon had moved out of his line of sight. Bringing her hand to his cheek, she let out a shuddering sigh. "Cash."

His name on her lips was the sweetest music. Promise and possibility. Desire and sweet heat all wrapped into a husky lilt. And her eyes. No one had ever looked at him with that kind of intensity. Raw vulnerability and determination lasering right to his soul.

"What is it? What happened?" he whispered, his voice a husk. "Talk to me."

Her answer was everything he expected and at the same time, a total surprise. He saw it coming as if in slow motion but was powerless to stop it, not that he wanted to. He'd waited his whole life for this moment. Her lips against his were tentative at first, as if she were waiting for him to stop her. Or take over. Everything in him stilled, expectation pounding in his veins. It would be so easy to press her into the hay and ravish her in the manner he'd imagined. Lick her and suck her, caress her to heights until she cried his name in ecstasy.

But as her mouth moved more insistently, she pulled him under her spell, and he tightened his embrace with a groan, giving in to her lead, sweeping his tongue inside her mouth. She tasted like sunshine and sugar. She shifted, straddling his lap, deepening their kiss, pulling him closer. Her essence seeped into the cracks of his soul like healing ointment, and fire grew in his veins, stiffening his cock as she rocked against him.

He stroked down her back, grabbing her ass, squeezing her lush curves, and notching her right against his erection straining against his zipper. God, he wanted to be inside her, to lose himself in her.

But no… his damned conscience chastised. Not like this. He couldn't take advantage of her like this when she was vulnerable and clearly broken up about something. Reluctantly, he broke the kiss, pulling away, breathing harshly.

Her eyes had grown wild. Lust-crazed. She pressed herself against him, rocking against his dick, tongue flicking along the inside of his lip, begging for more. Fuck, he was only human, and she was so goddamned gorgeous and sweet. Her sweetness shattered him. He craved it like a man in the desert starved for water. With a low growl, he took over, plundering her mouth, dying a little as she met him halfway, hands slipping under his coat and pulling his shirt from his jeans.

Her kisses were heady. Intoxicating. He pulled on her shirt, seeking the softness beneath, and was rewarded with the sweetest sigh when he found it. He skated his fingers across her ribs, to the swell of her breast, seeking and finding a nipple, caressing and pulling it into a tight peak beneath the silky fabric of her bra. Her head dropped back. "Yessss," she hissed softly. "I've waited so long for this."

Her words acted like an ice bath. In an instant, a flood of memories chilled his veins. He couldn't do that. For both their sakes. She'd only get hurt, and he'd be powerless to help her. He set her off his lap. "We. Can't. I'm sorry," he murmured, unable to look at her for fear of what he'd see in her eyes. "I'd only hurt you. And you're too sweet."

"But, Cash—"

He shook his head, scrubbing a hand over his face, chest burning. "You don't know what you're asking. People always end up hurt around me. I'm sorry, sweetheart." He brushed a final kiss on her temple and scrambled out of the loft as fast as he could.

By the time he reached the trailer, he'd broken out in a cold sweat. What had he been thinking? He was too messed up for her. It was only a matter of time before he froze again, and next time it might cost her life. And he couldn't live with himself if he hurt a sweet thing like Kate.

CHAPTER 12

"ROUGH NIGHT?" TRAVIS loomed over him holding a cup of coffee.

Cash closed his eyes, bracing against the memory of Kate's mouth, her skin under his fingers. "Yeah," he bit out. "You could say that."

"Wanna talk about it?"

"Not really."

"Something trigger you? This is the first time since we've come home from the trek that you've camped out on the couch."

"Nothing specific." Except a blazing kiss that turned him inside out. "I... just couldn't be alone last night. Too many memories." God's truth. He'd reached his trailer and realized he was too wound up. So he'd turned around and made a beeline for the main house, knowing it was his only chance for sleep. Childhood memories jumbled with his time overseas, tumbled with a laundry list of failures since he returned home, added up to a sleepless night filled with shakes and sweat. For whatever reason, knowing someone was close by, able to pull him back to sanity, held the terrors at bay. Cash pushed himself up. "That coffee for me?"

"Hell, no." Travis laughed. "Get your sorry ass up and serve yourself."

"Yes, sir." He swung his legs to the floor, standing. God,

he ached like he'd walked all night then folded himself into a foxhole to wait until sundown. Coffee would help.

"Don't take too long. Hope Sinclaire's coming over with a new mustang today. She wants us to help her sensitize it to sudden noise and motion."

Cash froze, sugar spoon midair.

"I think you should be in the ring with her."

"No," Cash said flatly, tipping in the sugar and stirring so vigorously the coffee slopped over the rim.

"What if I gave you a direct order?"

"I'd say fuck you, asshole. We're not in the service anymore."

"I cut your paycheck."

Cash slammed down the mug, spilling hot liquid across his hand, and glared at Travis. Travis didn't flinch. He was fucking immovable. Anger burst through him like a geyser. "So you're gonna fire me if I don't get in the ring today? Is that what you're saying?" His voice rose, but he didn't care.

Travis arched a brow, jaw set. "I'll remind you my wife and son are still upstairs sleeping."

"I'm not getting in the ring," Cash insisted.

"You need to."

"Like hell I do," he growled, adrenaline making his hands tingle.

Travis circled the couch, draining his mug and gently placing it on the counter next to his. He'd pissed Travis off. His left eye twitched, his only tell. Cash might outweigh Travis, but there was a reason Travis had been their leader. The man was fucking deadly, and nothing, *nothing* rattled him. "Like hell you don't?" Travis challenged coolly. "Let's start with how you tackled Kate the first night we were home."

"She told you that?" How could she? *How could she not,* the voice of reason answered.

"She told Elaine, who told me." Travis raised his hand. "Let me be clear. She was concerned about you. That's all. And rightfully so."

Damn.

Travis crossed his arms, widening his stance. "Have there been any other incidents since you came home?"

Cash shook his head, heat crawling up his spine. "Just the one," he answered, the fight leaving him.

"And you don't think this is something you should address?"

He dragged his gaze up. Throat so tight he couldn't speak. It wasn't fair. Travis had his shit together, and he was so... *weak.* Pitiful. Pathetic. God, he wanted to be sick.

"Don't go there," Travis said sharply, as if reading his mind. "Don't do it. We all struggle. You think I haven't been right where you are?"

He shook his head.

"You're wrong. I have been. Ask Elaine. Ask Weston."

Weston was another member of their SEAL team and now Prairie's police chief. According to Travis, the whole set-up for Resolution Ranch had been Weston's idea.

"Get this through your thick skull, sailor. We all have baggage. We all have shit to face. Every. Single. One of us. You're not a goddamned unicorn. You know what separates us from the rest? We don't run. Not from the enemy, not from our shit. So suck it the fuck up and meet me in the ring in forty-five minutes." Travis's gaze was diamond-hard. He wasn't fucking around. "Or pack your bags." He turned on his heel and strode out the door, letting it swing shut behind him.

Motherfucker.

Cash grabbed the back of his head, blowing out a ragged breath. In all the years they'd served together, Travis had never dressed him down like that. *We don't run.* Jesus, he'd done nothing but run since he'd returned home. His chest was so tight he couldn't breathe. He was sick of running. Sick of being afraid of the memories hovering at the edge of his conscious. He grabbed the coffee pot, clenching his arm to quell the shaking in his hand, and topped off his mug. Pulling in a shallow breath, he spooned in more sugar, focusing on nothing but stirring.

Second by second. Until he could manage minute by minute.

He reached for a paper towel, sopping up his spill. Extending his hand, he held it over his mug, slowly breathing in and out until it stopped shaking. Then he gulped down the contents of his mug, not caring that it scalded his throat. He relished the pain. It was a sensation other than panic. This was the end of the line. Travis didn't dish out ultimatums for shits and grins. This was do or die time.

He thought of his mom. All she'd suffered when he was a kid. She had a nice life now. A small bungalow in Florida, not far from the beach, with a man who treated her right, and who he was proud to call step-dad. And what about Kate? She'd suffered. Was still suffering, from the looks of it. And even though he hadn't been able to put the pieces together as to why she was here, he could see she was trying. He didn't want to die.

He didn't want to go on like this, either.

He grabbed the pot again, pouring out another steaming measure. He gulped it down without the aid of sugar, wincing at the bitter burn. God help him, he didn't want to get in that arena. What if he fell apart in front of witnesses? Cracked wide open, spilling his guts into the dirt? Then what? Could he survive the shame of it? He was a fucking warrior for God's sake. Shit was supposed to be easy for him. He was supposed to carry others. Not the other way around. He dragged in a breath, sweat pooling at the base of his skull. But one thing was certain, if he packed his bags and walked off the property, he would die. It would be too easy to end things.

Today he faced his demons.

Placing his mug in the sink, then tossing the wet paper towel in the trash, he glanced at the door and laughed. If he was going to die one way or another, he wouldn't take the coward's way out. He'd stand in the arena and die battling whatever shit rained down on him.

Forty minutes and a hot shower later, he paced the edge of the paddock as Hope pulled up with a horse trailer. Travis came up next to him, clapping a hand on his shoulder. "You're gonna be just fine."

"I'm not so sure."

Travis speared him with a hard look. "I am. I don't choose quitters."

Hope approached. "Ready?"

Not remotely, but Cash gulped and nodded. "Yep."

She looked to Travis. "Who's gonna be in the ring?"

Travis cocked his head toward him. "This guy. But I'll be here to help with noise."

"Great." She turned to Cash. "So we'll go through the same process of joining up, just like you did with Samson. Once you and Molly have established some trust, we'll start working on the sensitizing."

"Molly?"

"Yep," Hope nodded. "As in the unsinkable Molly Brown. Molly's had a rough time. She doesn't easily trust people, and she's still skittish. But once she's connected with you, she's a gem. Once we get her fully trained, she'll be a great mount. We just have to have faith in her so she can have faith in herself."

Cash hid a smile. He wasn't sure he believed Hope's mumbo-jumbo about horses having faith in themselves. But she got great results, so he wouldn't knock it too hard. She understood horses better than most. And he was grateful to her for pairing him with Samson.

Hope led a beautiful bay off the trailer. Her coloring ran nearly black on her withers and down her legs. Cash followed at a respectful distance, not wanting to spook the horse. The gate closed behind him with a heavy clang. A gong sounding the start of battle.

Hope crossed the arena, holding Molly's halter and lead line. "We're gonna start from scratch here. Molly's worked with my brother a few times, but besides me, that's it." She offered him the equipment. "You remember what to do?"

Cash nodded. "I don't make eye contact, and I invite her to circle."

"Exactly. Ready?"

"As I'll ever be." He left Hope and crossed to within a few feet of Molly. "Hey, girl," he called softly. "We're gonna get through this today, you and me."

Molly pawed the ground, a sign that she was uncomfortable. That made two of them. He held out his hands and stepped toward her. She started circling with a leap. It was clear to Cash within a few minutes that she was much greener than Samson. Had he been this skittish at first, too? Probably.

They circled and circled. Then circled some more. The sun rose higher in the sky. Cash didn't think they'd progress beyond this, but Hope kept encouraging him. Finally, Molly slowed to a walk and dropped her head, chewing and licking.

"That's it, Cash. Turn and walk away. Don't look over your shoulder."

He turned and walked to the center of the arena. Sure enough, Molly followed.

"Now stop, turn, and give her praise."

Cash turned, startled the horse was right behind him, and he reached up to pet her in the same place he knew Samson liked. "You're a good girl, Molly. You're a good girl, will you let me put the halter on you?"

He raised a hand, half expecting her to bolt. But she accepted the halter.

"Excellent," Hope called. "So first we're going to start her with stuff she's used to, scratches along her flank, abdomen, and thighs."

Together they worked on touch, simulating grass and twigs. They quickly progressed to motion and low-level noise – using weighted flags, branches, and flags on long arms. The sun climbed higher.

Cash did okay with movement on the ground and light noise. Flapping tarps, and movement simulating snakes. But the second he caught a movement out of his periphery, he froze for a split second, air stopping in his lungs. Molly froze too.

Hope dropped the flag and approached, eyes full of concern. "You okay? You tensed up, and then Molly did, too."

Damn straight, he did. "I'll be okay."

"Try again?"

Dread crawled up his spine. "Yeah, sure." He removed his Stetson to wipe the back of his hand across his forehead, then gave Molly a pat. "Scared you too, huh?"

Before he was ready, Hope tossed a weighted flag at them.

He jumped out of the way, and Molly did the same, nickering and dancing backward. "Hey," he snapped. "You were supposed to warn me."

"No. I wasn't. You don't get a warning on the trail, or in the pasture."

They continued to work, and just when he thought he couldn't take it anymore, Hope called it. "Time's up. We'll start again after a rest. I've got sports drinks by the gate."

Hope moved in to attend to Molly while Cash made for the edge of the arena, suddenly realizing how thirsty he was. He twisted the cap off a bottle, and tipped his head back, draining the contents in under a minute.

Travis joined him, and Cash was drawn to the whip in his hand. "What the hell is that?"

"This?" Travis lifted his hand, then flashed Cash a grin. "Your reckoning."

He grew hot just looking at it. "Anyone ever tell you you're a crazy motherfucker?"

"Takes one to know one."

His stomach hollowed. He was really going to do this. Crawl into the ring with a barely tamed animal and subject himself to loud noises. Hell, yeah, it took one to know one. He didn't have a screw loose, he must have lost it over in the sandbox.

"Let's get this over with." Pulse thrumming double-time, he stepped back into the ring.

Molly laid her ears back and pawed the ground as he approached. Hope glanced at him sharply. "You're making her nervous. Slow your breathing, and look at her feet."

Cash took a steadying breath. "I don't know if I can do this," he murmured.

"You can, and you and Molly are going to help each

other. Be brave, Cash. If not for yourself, then for Molly. In order for her to be a functional horse on a ranch, she has to learn that loud noises aren't predators, they're just loud noises. And she needs to be able to trust the humans around her to keep her safe. We're her last hope, Cash. She's been adopted twice. She can't go back. And no one will take her."

"So it's do or die time for her."

She nodded. "Yeah. It's up to us now."

Hope grabbed his hand. "Just lower your head, shut your eyes, and stand with me for a few minutes. Get in tune with your surroundings, and when you're able, listen for Molly's breathing and match yours to it. Just like I taught you with Samson."

His mind raced. Fear, panic, guilt, shame, all warring for supremacy in his body. But then slowly, he was able to bring his attention to the warmth of Hope's hand. And next, to the bird calls and the way the wind rattled through the bare branches. Finally, to Molly. Hope placed his hand on Molly's neck. "Keep your eyes shut," she said quietly.

After a minute, he felt Molly's neck soften, and the tension drained out of his shoulders.

"There," Hope said. "Did you feel that?"

He nodded.

"She trusts you right now. Take her lead line and let's walk with her."

They circled the arena once, twice. And then it happened.

He caught the motion out of the corner of his eyes, and tensed as the string of firecrackers exploded. *SNAP, CRACK, Snapsnapsnap, CRACKCRAK.*

Molly reared, yanking the line from his hand, and bolted to the far side of the arena.

Cash exploded. "Jesus Christ, did you have to do that?

What the fuck?" His ears buzzed with adrenaline. Fuck. Hot tears choked him. What the fuck kind of sick game were they playing?

"Are you still standing?" Travis called from the fence.

"No thanks to you." His breath came in harsh puffs. He glanced across the arena. "And look what you did to the horse."

Hope was already with Molly, speaking in soothing tones, stroking the horse's neck. He joined her, and together they soothed the horse. "I'm not sure this is a good idea. For either of us."

"Sorry about that. She'll pick up on body language you don't even know you have. If you brace for the noise, she'll learn to associate noise with danger. Remember the whole point of pressure and release is that they learn to let go of their fear. She'll be fine. We're going to make sure of it."

Forget the horse, he wasn't sure he'd be fine.

"I'm right here, Cash," Kate called softly from across the paddock.

He swung toward her, meeting her gaze. She should be punishing him with her silence after the way he left her last night. He'd seen the disappointment in her eyes when he'd made the mistake of glancing back at her as he climbed down from the loft. But instead, she looked fresh and sweet, and her eyes shone with absolute faith in him.

His chest burned and he studied the dirt on his boots. He stood at the edge of a bottomless chasm, toes hanging over the edge. He should give into the pull and fall into the abyss. Let the darkness take him. His throat closed, as the feelings pressed in on him from all sides. He didn't deserve kindness. Certainly not her faith. It was too much.

"I'm not going anywhere. Promise."

Kate's voice sounded like a beacon. Reaching him like a pinpoint of light in the black. A tightness he'd held onto for far too long loosened inside him. She had no reason to believe in him, yet her face told a different story. As did the faces of Travis and Hope. Letting them down would be worse than quitting. They were counting on him. Hell, Molly was counting on him. He wasn't going to let her be shipped off to the glue factory. She was innocent in all this, let down by her humans. Well, this human was not letting her down. No matter how scared he got in the ring. He shot Kate a grateful nod, deepening his resolve to lick his fear, once and for all.

By the end of the session, he was sweaty and exhausted, but both he and Molly had made progress. They'd stood together in the middle of the ring, he leaning against Molly, with an arm over her neck, eyes shut and successfully managed balloon popping at random intervals and distances. Car honking came next, then wood snapping, cap guns, and finally skeet shooting.

Travis met him at the edge of the arena. "Good work in there. I know it was hard. It will take time, but you and Molly will get there."

Cash blew out a breath, accepting the sports drink Travis offered. "Thanks for setting me straight." Inch by laborious inch he felt like he was crawling out of his self-imposed darkness. Slowly coming into the light.

"You're worth it," Travis said. "I'm not going to lose another team member if I can help it."

Out of the corner of his eye, he saw Kate head for the barn. He jogged to catch up with her. "Kate, wait?"

She stopped and turned, face pink. He wanted nothing more than to gather her into his arms and lose himself in her sweetness. He stopped a few feet away. He probably stunk to high heaven anyway. He was drenched from the exertion in the ring.

"About last night."

Her face pinched. "I owe you an apology–"

"No, no. I owe you one. I reacted badly. *Again.*" All the things he wanted to say but didn't know how, ballooned in his chest, squeezing off his air. He swallowed hard. "I'd like to make it up to you. And explain myself. Can we try again? Over steak and potatoes tonight?"

CHAPTER 13

K ATE'S STOMACH FILLED with butterflies as she stepped out of her trailer. Cash had been so brave today. For him the struggle was real. Her own problems paled in comparison. She would do well to remember that as she put the pieces of her own life back together.

Her heart beat faster with every step that brought her closer to Cash's. Kissing Cash was... better than anything she'd ever imagined. Or written about in songs. The sensations he'd unleashed in her body made her nipples tingle just from the memory. No man had ever made her ache to be touched. Made her want so, so much more. She'd never been kissed like that, like a she was a sensuous woman. He'd kissed her like he'd wanted *her*. And when he'd slipped his fingers under her shirt... wetness rushed to her core at the thought of it.

But the way he blew hot and cold concerned her. Which Cash would answer the door? The man who looked at her with heat in his eyes? Or the tortured soul who battled demons in the arena and pushed her away when she got too close?

He opened the door as soon as she stepped on the bottom stair and she drew in a quick breath, awareness ballooning in her chest. He looked so good. Soft denim hugged his thighs, and he'd put on a white button down that pulled tight across his chest. The way his eyes lit made her want to crawl right into his lap, beard and all. She'd never kissed anyone with a beard before last night. It had been softer than she expected. She liked the way it tickled her cheek, her neck. Her mouth watered at the thought of kissing him again.

He extended his hand. "Hi."

She took it, electricity zinging through her at his touch, and let him pull her close, heart thumping wildly. Without even thinking about it, she tilted her head inviting him to kiss her like it was the most natural thing in the world. He didn't disappoint. Heat flooded her senses when his lips met hers, and her eyes fluttered shut. His mouth was soft, gentle, and she melted against him, vibrating with longing.

"So sweet," he murmured when he pulled away and tucked a strand of hair behind her ear. "I like your hair down."

She smiled up at him, warming all over at his compliment. "Thank you."

His eyes widened. "You can talk again?"

Grief pierced her, and she winced. "Yeah."

"That's not a good thing?"

She lifted a shoulder. "Yes, *no*. It's complicated."

Understanding filled his eyes. "Isn't everything?" He tugged on her hand. "Come inside?"

She stepped inside a perfect replica of her own trailer, but with one difference – his kitchen smelled heavenly. The aroma of garlic and steak hit her senses. Where had he learned to cook? So much she didn't know about this man. So much she wanted to learn.

Cash stepped to the stove. "Sit. Steaks are ready." He brought two plates to the table filled with steak, fries, and greens. "It's pretty simple," he said half-apologetically.

"I think it's amazing." And perfect for a real first date.

He pulled a chair up to the end of the table. "There's ketchup or steak sauce, if you prefer."

Kate laid a hand on his leg, enjoying that he was too big to squeeze in the narrow space across from her. "It's perfect," she answered, keeping her voice light. She cut into the steak and took a bite. She shut her eyes and groaned. It was perfectly done and well-seasoned. A steak after her own heart. When she opened her eyes, Cash was staring at her with heat in his eyes. Answering heat shot through her center, right to her panties. Her throat tightened as she held his gaze. After a long moment, she cleared her throat. "Where'd you learn to cook a steak like that?"

His eyes crinkled when he smiled. "My mom. She worked as a line cook at a truck stop when I was a kid. Said steak was the easiest thing to learn how to cook after scrambled eggs. So she taught me when I was about ten years old."

How would her life have been different if her mother had taught her something besides guilt? From the time she'd been a little girl, Helene had made it clear how much she'd given up for her daughter. And it didn't matter how successful Kate was, it was never enough to give her mother back the career she'd put aside when she'd unexpectedly become pregnant. "You're lucky."

Cash nodded. "Yeah, I am. My mom's great. She worked three jobs to make ends meet for us. But she always had time for me."

He kept her entertained while she ate, carrying the burden of the conversation, regaling her with stories of growing up in rural Maine, of spending summers in the woods, and of winters huddled around the stove.

Cash removed their plates to the sink and returned with a

stack of cards. "I know you probably have a lot of questions. And you deserve answers." He took her hand, lacing his fingers with hers, his face a mask. "And I have questions, too."

Kate's blood raced, stomach flipping.

"So I thought maybe the easiest way would be to play cards?"

"I don't follow." She cocked her head.

His eyes crinkled again, sparkling with humor. "I thought we could play war."

"War?" The kid's game? What was he playing at?

He nodded. "Yeah. Winner of each round gets to ask a question. Loser has to answer."

Fair enough, but fear settled in the pit of her stomach. What if she revealed too much? What if he pushed her away again? She drew in a deep breath, slowly releasing it. "Okay." He shuffled, then passed her the cards. She cut the deck and shuffled again, then dealt the stack. He looked straight at her, face tight. Her heart went to him. "We don't have to do this," she murmured. "We can just talk."

He shook his head, determination flashing in his eyes. "Nope." His hand hovered over the top of his stack. "Ready?"

She nodded.

"On three. One, two, three."

They flipped. She groaned inwardly. She'd drawn a four, Cash a seven. A devilish spark leapt into his eyes and he gave her a slow, knowing smile. Her heart leaped to her throat making it hard to breathe. She suddenly felt like she was walking a tightrope.

"Hey," he said softly, stroking a finger down her cheek. "Don't worry, we'll start off easy. Favorite color?"

Kate breathed out a sigh of relief. "Blue." She won the next round, and asked the same question, following his lead.

"Green. Like your eyes."

A thrill ran through her as she dropped her gaze, afraid he'd see how his answer had affected her. They quickly ran through a list of favorites, then moved to firsts. "First kiss?" She asked boldly, pulse racing.

He cocked his head, arching a brow. "Jenny Martin, sixth grade."

She was certain her eyes popped out of her skull. "*Sixth grade?* Did you like it?"

Cash's smile broadened. "You'll have to ask that on another round."

A few rounds later, he turned the tables, asking her the same question. "Trent Ridley, sixteen." She'd leave off the part that he was a guitarist in her band and twenty-two at the time. Or that her mother had discovered them and fired him on the spot.

"Did you like it?" Cash asked stiffly.

"Not nearly as much as I liked yours," she blurted, heating.

Cash's eyebrows shot up his forehead, and his eyes flared. Electricity arced between them. "That so?"

She swallowed, mouth going dry, and tore her gaze from him. She was entering dangerous territory here, and they hadn't even gotten to the tough questions. The ones she had about what put the tortured look she'd seen on his face on multiple occasions. The questions from him she hoped to avoid.

She flipped a card. Queen of spades.

Cash flipped. Queen of diamonds.

Her insides turned upside down as she raised her eyes. "What now?"

Cash drummed his fingers on the table, thinking. "Double or nothing? Winner gets to ask follow up questions."

"Let's go," she answered, her question already forming in her mind. She laid her cards down, and shut her eyes before she flipped the final card, sending a silent plea to the universe that she'd win. An Ace of Hearts faced up at her when she opened her eyes, handily beating Cash's eight of clubs. "What keeps you awake at night?" she asked, scooping the cards into her pile.

Cash regarded her steadily, a muscle in his neck ticking. After a long moment, he spoke. "You don't pull your punches, do you?"

"You can pass," she offered quietly.

He shook his head and rubbed his cheek. "What keeps me awake? Depends on the night. Most nights, it's the face of my friend Hamm. We were ambushed in a building we'd hunkered down in for the night. Bullet hit his neck instead of mine."

Kate thought she would be sick. She reached for Cash's hand. "I'm so very sorry." But her comment hadn't registered. He was clearly lost in a sea of memories.

He dropped his head with a sigh. "We lost three guys that night, but I was closest to Hamm. He was an only child like me, and he was like a brother."

Tears prickled behind Kate's eyes. Hamm's poor family. She couldn't imagine losing a child. But your only child? How did his parents manage? "How are his parents?"

"Helping to raise Hamm's son. Never made me so glad I didn't have kids."

"I don't understand."

Cash raised his head, puffing his cheeks as he blew out a breath. "I was married at the time. It didn't work out. I got a Dear Johnny letter not long after the ambush."

Married?!?

Kate reeled. He'd been married? And dumped while he was on a mission? What kind of a person would do that? Especially to someone like Cash? A million new questions popped into her head. "Do you miss her?" she whispered, bracing for the answer. Oh God, what if he did? What would she do then? The realization she'd developed feelings for this gentle giant pummeled her.

"Nope," he said flatly.

She exhaled the breath she'd been holding. "Did you love her?"

"Not like..." He shook his head. "I was devastated at the time, but we were young. Too young. Miranda liked the idea of being married to a SEAL far more than the reality. We made it just over a year, and half that time I was gone. I visited Hamm's family as soon as I got the chance. Seeing the grief on their faces every time they looked at Hamm's son made me glad I'd made different choices."

Miranda. A wave of jealousy roiled through Kate, fierce and hot, leaving a bitter taste in her mouth.

"What about you? Has your heart been broken?"

How to explain without giving away one of her biggest secrets? But the second she disclosed her identity, this fragile thing blossoming between them would evaporate. As soon as Kaycee Starr came between them, he'd stop seeing her, Kate. Her indecision must have shown on her face, because he reached out and tipped her chin, forcing her to look right at him.

"Is that why you were crying last night? Did someone break your heart?" She was heartbroken, but not for the reason he thought. "I... it's complicated." His face fell. Shit. To keep one secret, she'd have to disclose the other, embarrassing as it was. She took a deep breath. "I've never had a boyfriend. I... tonight... I guess you could call this my first date." She twisted out of his grip, shutting her eyes, unable to bear looking at him a second longer. Her cheeks flamed. Her skin crawled from the shame of it. She stood. "I should go." She looked around the room, anywhere but at him. "Thank you for a nice evening."

He stood too, catching her shoulder and turning her back. "Wait. Please don't go? I don't want you to go."

She pressed her cold hands to her cheeks. They were still on fire.

He took her hands, encasing them with his enormous ones. "You have nothing to be embarrassed about, Kate."

"I have plenty." She shook her head, dropping her gaze. "I'm pathetic."

"Look at me, Kate," he commanded gently.

Reluctantly, she forced her eyes up, unable to breathe.

"Just so I'm clear, you've never..."

Another wave of shame rippled through her as she shook her head. This was *not* how she'd ever imagined their conversation going. How could she ever look at him again after tonight? But he lowered his head, so his mouth was a whisper from hers. If she shifted her weight to her toes, they'd be touching. His breath was warm and soft on her cheek, and she breathed him in. His masculine scent underneath the soapy clean went straight to her head like moonshine. Her nerve endings fired in anticipation, sending violent ripples all the way to her toes.

"You have no idea how that turns me on," he whispered.

She pulled her head back a fraction to study him. He gazed down at her through hooded eyes, a fire there that made her ache with want. She wanted his mouth on her, his hands.

Her nipples were tight peaks, straining against her bra, and she was pretty sure there was nothing left of her panties.

"I promise. We can do whatever you want. Go as slow as you like, or do nothing at all. Just say the word." His mouth brushed hers in the barest of kisses. She vibrated from the intensity of it all. There was something so deeply erotic in his touch. The sureness of it, the question in it, the promise of it.

"I–" She leaned in, pressing her mouth to his, surprised by her boldness, shocked by how natural it felt. "I want you to make me come."

CHAPTER 14

"*I WANT YOU to make me come.*"

Cash's throat went dry, his cock instantly rock hard. A wave of possessiveness like he'd never experienced, rolled through him. He wanted this woman more than he'd wanted anyone.

But what happened when she learned who he was?

Would she feel he'd betrayed her? The truth was bound to come out, and he didn't feel right keeping something so important from her. But he'd confessed enough tonight, and his emotions were running high. For one blissful moment, he wanted to lose himself in her. Wanted her to see him as he was right now, without the shame of the past hanging around his neck like a millstone. And he desperately wanted to make her come. A thousand different ways, with his fingers, his mouth, and yes, with his cock. His cock jerked, pressing painfully against his jeans, wanting in on the action. And God, but she would be sweet. So hot and tight. The ache in his balls tightened. If this had truly been a first date of sorts, then the likelihood of her having never fooled around with someone was fairly high.

With a growl, he swept her into his arms and carried her the four steps to his bedroom, setting her on the edge of the bed. He dropped down next to her, angling his body so he faced her. "I'll be gentle. But if it's too much, or you get scared, just tell me to stop."

"I would never be scared with you, Cash."

"I want this to be good for you."

The smile she gave him arrowed straight into his heart. "I know it will be." She cupped the back of his neck, pulling him close and offering her mouth. She was entirely without guile. So innocent and so fucking hot. He took her mouth, starting slow, letting her set the pace, but in seconds it was clear she wanted more, and he deepened the kiss, following her lead. With a groan, he swept his tongue into her sweet mouth. She tasted even better than the night before. Her hands fluttered across his shoulders, down his chest, back up to the top button on his shirt.

Keeping his mouth on hers because he wasn't going to let it go for a second, he helped her with the buttons on his shirt, pulling the tail out of his jeans and shrugging out of it. A little moan came from her throat as she explored him with a light touch that drove him nearly out of his mind. She slipped a finger inside the front of his waistband. He would die to have her hand wrapped around his cock, but not yet. If they carried on like this, he'd leave her high and dry, and that was *not* happening.

He trailed kisses down her neck, nuzzling the sensitive skin at her collarbone. He caught the faintest hint of hay on her skin. "Can I take off your shirt?"

She dropped her head, giving him more access to the creamy column of her throat. "Oh God, yes. Please."

Her hands flew to the buttons, but he pushed them away. "Let me."

He kissed the hollow at her throat, sweeping his tongue out to taste her while he released the first button. He trailed kisses down her center, licking and nipping as he gently pushed her back on the bed, exposing more of her skin. Her flesh came alive under his mouth, pebbling and flushing the palest shade of pink. When the last button came undone, he brushed the shirt away. Her nipples strained against her bra, and he could just make out their dusky pink color underneath the white lace. He couldn't wait to take one in his mouth. Would her nipples be sensitive? Would she let out another throaty moan when he gently bit? "You're perfection," he murmured, tracing a finger from her throat to her belly button.

She lifted her head, eyes filled with doubt. "I'm broken," she whispered.

"We're all broken," he whispered back, catching his breath at the wave of emotion that engulfed him. "Let me show you how amazing you are." He lowered his head, wetting the swell of her breast with his tongue, reveling in its satiny smoothness. Then, licking down, he worked over the tip, wetting the fabric, while he took the other nipple between thumb and forefinger. He pinched gently as he took the other into his mouth, sucking.

"Yessss," she hissed, head dropping back, lost in the sensation.

"More?" he murmured into her flesh.

"Yes," she said more forcefully.

"Take off your bra, sweetheart."

She dropped to an elbow, freeing the clasp, then shrugged off the straps. He hooked a finger under one and pulled, helping her slip it off. His blood thrummed as he gazed down at her. Regardless of her protests, she was perfection. Creamy round flesh, perfectly able to fit in his hand. And in the center, dusky beads, waiting for his mouth.

"Lie back."

She looked at him, cheeks turning pink. "Where do I put my hands?"

"Anywhere you like. No rules except your pleasure."

Her eyes gleamed. "Can I put them there?" Her eyes darted to the bulge in his jeans.

He laughed and grinned. "Patience, grasshopper. You touch me, and I won't last."

Her eyes grew big. "Really?"

He took her hand, and placed it over his erection, gritting his teeth from the added friction. "Feel that?" he asked tightly. "How hard I am for you? How much you turn me on?"

"Ooooooh," she breathed, running her hand down his length and giving a little squeeze.

His vision spotted, and he laced his fingers with hers, bringing it over her head, cock protesting with a jerk. He claimed her mouth again, tracing her hairline then her cheeks. She kissed him back like a woman possessed, dragging her fingers through his hair. Returning to her breasts, he pulled a bud into his mouth, flicking the tip with his tongue and sucking until she arched into him, crying out.

"Do you like that?"

"More," she answered hoarsely.

With a chuckle, he complied, moving between the two until she writhed beneath him and her breath came in harsh gasps. Shifting up, he took her mouth and rolled onto his back, bringing her to rest on top of him. As he slowed their kiss, he filled his hands with her luscious ass as she rocked into him. His cock was in the most incredible agony, feeling her move against him. How much better would it be when he was finally inside her? He'd wait for that bliss as long as she needed. "Do you want me to take off your pants?"

She raised her head, eyes dark and filled with lust. "Do

you have to ask?"

"Yes. Always," he murmured.

"Then yes, I want them off *now*." She rolled off him, hands working her zipper.

He moved over her, pulling off her boots as she pushed her jeans over her hips. When her pants joined the pile of clothing on the floor, he pushed open her knees, sliding a hand up the silky length of her thigh. "So beautiful," he murmured.

His gut pulled tight at the sight of her. He recognized the blush pink panties from the laundry, modest in shape but made from gauzy lace so he could see her triangle of curls. So much more beautiful on her than he'd imagined. Bracing his arms on either side of her hips, he lowered his head, nuzzling the soaked fabric, and inhaling her essence deeply. The sweet, musky scent shot straight to his soul. He'd never been hungry like this for a woman in his life, or so hard. He placed a kiss on her mound, relishing her gasp and the way her legs tensed. He hooked a finger underneath her panties and twisted, tugging one side over her hip bone. "Yes?"

"Yeeess." She moaned, helping him remove the last barrier to her body.

He paused, his own breathing ragged. He raked his gaze over her. Fucking incredible. Her body was flushed from head to toe, and when she raised her head, her eyes glittered brightly with anticipation. But it was her pussy that captivated him. Sweet pink lips peeked out from a thatch of deep blonde curls, swollen and glistening with her arousal. He grazed her seam with the back of a finger, coating it with her desire.

Kate's mouth dropped open with a gasp, and she opened herself to his touch. He swept a finger back and forth until she let out a little cry. Heart pounding, he dipped inside her seam, sweeping up to circle her clit. Her hips bucked and she collapsed backward. "Ohh, Cash. That feels so good."

"I'm just getting started, babe." He continued to stroke back and forth. "If you don't like something, tell me."

Her face was the picture of lust. "I fucking love this, Cash. I don't want you to stop," she muttered fiercely.

A laugh rumbled low in his belly. "Just checking, sweetheart." He slipped a finger inside her, moving slowly, and quickly she picked up on the rhythm, moving her hips in time. She was tight, and he moved gently, gradually going deeper. Dropping to an elbow, he returned to her breast, taking a nipple, moving his tongue in the same rhythm. Her breath came in pants now, and he touched a thumb to her clit, feeling the moment she exploded around him as her walls gripped his finger and she shattered with a cry. He kept moving, letting her ride out the sensation, then moved to kiss her.

"That was, that was… wow," she said when they broke apart.

"Not done yet."

"You mean there's more?" Her eyes lit eagerly.

He raised his eyebrows, smiling, and kissing a trail to her mound. "Second course," he spoke into her damp skin, surrounded by the scent of her arousal. "I can't get enough of your gorgeous pussy." He pressed a kiss to her inner thigh, licking a path to the object of his desire. Then he licked through her folds, lapping up her sweet essence and moving back and forth over her sensitized clit.

Kate clutched his head and arched into him with a cry. "*Ohmygod I* Love *that.*"

He smiled against her, redoubling his efforts, licking and sucking as her legs trembled beneath him. She was so wet, so aroused, he was covered in her, and he fucking loved it. Loved the way her hips moved against his face, her little cries, the way she thrashed her head back and forth as she gasped for air. Leaving her clit, he speared his tongue into the heart of her, teasing and tasting, driving her higher and higher. Then he pressed two fingers into her, pausing to give her time to adjust, then slowly moving deeper when her hips began to push forward. As he thrust, he sealed his mouth around her clit, lapping her tight bud over and over as he curled his fingers against her G-spot. When she came a second time, her cry was long and loud, and she pulled his hair as her body shook from the release. Only superhuman effort stopped him from joining her. He held her as she came back to earth.

"But what about you, Cash?" she asked when her breathing had returned to normal. She placed a tentative hand against him.

"Don't worry about me, babe." In spite of himself, he rolled into her hand, loving the feel of it. "This was about you."

"But I- I..." She flushed bright pink and raised her eyes to meet his. "I want to touch you."

Cash forgot to breathe. "Oh, fuck, hon. I want that too, but we don't have to."

"Stop trying to protect me," she hissed, hurt flashing in her eyes. "Do you not want me?"

"Oh baby, I want you so bad it hurts."

She ran her hand against his length again. "Then please? Please let me make you feel good too?"

His resolve vanished. How could he say no to her? Not when he wanted it as much as she did. He rolled off the bed, and stood, dropping his pants and shorts in one move and stepping out. Baring himself to her with his heart in his throat. He felt as vulnerable with her as he had in the ring earlier that morning. He heated under her slow inspection, and she rose to her knees, moving to the edge of the bed, reaching out a finger to trace a jagged scar along his left side.

"You got hurt," she murmured.

"I survived."

Her face softened. "I'm so glad."

"Kate." His voice came out strangled. The emotions coursing through him nearly overwhelmed him. "Sweetheart, I know you wanna make this good for me, and I love that." He dragged in a breath, feeling like he was about to fall off a cliff. "But it's already been good for me. Amazing. You've burned me up, and fair warning, I won't last long."

"I don't care," she breathed as she leaned back, looking down between their bodies.

His cock bobbed eagerly, fully engorged, and jutting proudly in front of him. Her mouth made a perfect O as she stared first at it, then dragged her eyes up to meet his, then back down. His cock throbbed painfully as he imagined that perfect O wrapped around him, taking him all the way in. She looked up again, eyes hungry, and she dropped a hand to his hip, fingers skating down until they hit the base of his cock. Electricity raced up the back of his legs, pulling his belly tight. He was so fucking close.

She slid a finger along his shaft, smiling with approval as she smeared the pre-come over his engorged head. "Jesus, Kate," he groaned through a clenched jaw. "Put your hand around me."

"Like this?" she asked breathlessly. Her hand didn't quite make it around his base, but it didn't matter, because when she gently pulled upward, his eyes rolled into his skull. "Oh, yeah. Like that. Fuck that's amazing."

She squeezed him a little harder and leaned her head against him, kissing his collarbone. She nuzzled his neck, and her teeth grazed his skin. Her hand felt amazing, but it was the bite that sent him over the edge. He came with a roar, pulling her tight and bracing his legs against the bed as his vision went black. He found her mouth, taking it in a ruthless, claiming kiss as he rode out the final waves of his release, his come jetting out in hot spurts, between them.

"Wow, that was hot," she said with a giggle after a long while.

He eyed her. "Yeah?"

She nodded biting her lip.

"Wait here." He crossed to the other end of the trailer and grabbed a washcloth wetting it with hot water.

When he returned, he washed her off, then himself, tossing it in his hamper. Pulling down the sheets, he lifted the corner. "Lie down with me?"

Her gaze warmed, and she nodded, crawling in front of him. He slipped in behind her, wrapping his arms around her and pulling her back to his front.

She twisted around. "Cash?"

"Mmmhmm?"

"Thank you."

The words *I love you* bubbled up from the deepest part of him, but he bit them back before he made a fool of himself. He couldn't possibly love her. She certainly couldn't love him. They barely knew each other. And too many secrets stood between them. Yet, the feeling was there. As clear as day. "Stay?" He kissed her head. "Please?" He hadn't spent an entire night with a woman since he'd divorced. He hadn't wanted to. But lying with Kate like this? Felt so right.

She rolled over, kissing the hollow at the base of his neck, and turned back around, snuggling into him. Something slid home inside him. She murmured something as she drifted off, and while he couldn't quite hear it, he swore it sounded a helluva lot like "Love you, Cash."

CHAPTER 15

KATE WOKE WITH words dancing through her head.

I was young, I was reckless. Didn't know then what I know now — that love's a fickle lady, better stake your claim when she comes dancing in. You better hold on, hold on.

She sat up with a gasp, sheets falling to her waist. She'd been without words since before the business with the crazy fan. They often came in snippets like this, but the snippet was always the kernel the song grew from. Scanning the room, she looked for a piece of paper, a scrap, anything. Nothing.

Shutting her eyes, Kate went over the words again, a hint of a tune hovering just out of reach. She had to write it down. She pushed Cash on the shoulder. "Cash," she whispered. "I need a piece of paper."

Cash answered with a sigh and a stretch, possessively laying an arm across her lap.

"Cash," she jostled him harder.

He answered with a rumble.

Craptastic. It had been so long since the words had come, she'd quit carrying a notebook with her. Gingerly slipping out from under the covers, she tiptoed around the bed. "Paper, paper, paper, where is the paper?" she chanted to herself as she scanned the side table next to the couch. The first drawer in the kitchen held only a few pieces of silverware and some utensils. The second, potholders and aluminum foil. "C'mon.

Everyone has a junk drawer in the kitchen," she mumbled.

She struck gold with the last drawer. She grabbed a take-out menu from Gino's, and dug until she found a sharpie. Once she'd scribbled the words in the margins, she folded the menu and tiptoed back to the bedroom. Cash sat waiting with a scowl on his face. "Running out?"

She shook her head. "Not at all."

He glanced at the menu, then back to her, eyes narrowed. "I think Gino's is closed."

"I – I had to write something down before I forgot it."

He raised an eyebrow. Shit. *Shitshitshit.* He looked at her like he *knew.* But he couldn't possibly.

"Need a pen?"

"Found one." Her pulse hammered in her ears.

He stretched out a hand. "Come back to bed, then," he said, voice gravelly.

Her knees went rubbery from relief, and she tossed the menu on her jeans, and crawled back into his embrace.

Cash pulled her down on his chest, smoothing back her hair, caressing her cheek with the back of his hand. "Sleep okay?"

"Like a baby."

His eyes crinkled. "Me too." He nuzzled her, beard tickling the sensitive spot at the base of her neck. Tingles of awareness raced to her toes. "I'd keep you in bed all day if I could."

The invitation in his voice lit a fire inside her, as did his growing erection pressing into her thigh. She rolled her hips against him. "I'd like that too." Her body still hummed from last night. She'd written about ecstasy, about two souls soaring to the sky, but she'd never realized until last night what it could be like. She'd die a happy woman if she could spend every day making music and getting naked with Cash. And there was still more to experience. "No chance we could play hooky, is there?" She already knew the answer, but wanted him to know she was willing.

He placed a kiss on her jaw. "Nope. But I'm not doing anything after supper tonight."

She lifted her brows. "Yeah?"

He raised his in answer.

"I'd like that. Very much."

He tightened his embrace. "Me, too. Very much."

"THANKS SO MUCH, Kate," Elaine said as she put away the last of the breakfast dishes. "I'm so grateful for an extra pair of hands. I hope you'll consider staying after the baby comes." She patted her belly. "It's so nice to have another woman on the property."

Kate returned the woman's smile. "I'll think about it. I like it here." In her heart of hearts, she knew she couldn't stay. Sooner or later, she'd have to return home and face the press. And her mother. But now that she'd had a taste of a normal life, one without the frenzy of the press, and the constant pressure to come up with new material, a new look, a new show, she was dragging her feet.

And she didn't want to leave Cash. Not after last night. It was crazy to feel attached to him, but she couldn't help it. Even if he pushed her away again, she'd push right back. Cash was special.

Kate hiked back to her trailer, words tumbling through her head. A song was itching to be born. She couldn't ignore it any longer. But she couldn't write in such a confined space. At home, she wrote on her covered porch, overlooking the meadow and the pond. And if a chill hung in the air, she'd take her guitar to the barn and sing to the horses. She might not be able to sing, but she could slip unnoticed into the barn and try to capture the song lurking just out of reach.

She made a thermos of hot tea, stuffed a small notebook and Gino's take-out menu into her coat pocket, grabbed her guitar and headed for the barn. She stopped only once, just across the yard from the barn, to watch Travis and Cash and their day help framing the foreman's house. She liked observing Cash unawares. He threw himself into his work, whether it was mucking stalls, or hammering nails. There wasn't anything he couldn't do.

He was like a freaking mountain man, strong and capable with muscles for days and a rough, rugged edge to him that lit her up. But gentle in all the right ways. Like the way he made her body sing… Heat flashed through her. It might be early March, but she wouldn't need her coat if she stood there much longer.

With a reluctant sigh, she turned and slipped into the barn, heading for the far corner where she shoveled fresh hay. Her feet made the barest echo on the floor, and the quiet settled over her like an old familiar blanket. She settled herself on a hay bale, tea at her feet, and let her mind wander as she pulled out her guitar. Her fingers moved over the strings, plucking and strumming at random intervals as she let the music in her head wash over her.

Her best songs came as a gift. Others were born out of hard work. But in either case, there was always a period of nebulousness, of chaos swirling over the firmament, so to speak. A tendril of fear twisted her gut. She'd always sung through the fragments until she had a song. Could she write a song without that? Should she try to sing? Fear blossomed into dread. And sorrow.

She didn't know how to do anything else. Except take care of horses. And yes, she was lucky, she could afford to retire, but what would she *do?* She'd been performing for over a decade. And she'd never made a career choice without her mother. Strike that, she'd never had a choice. Her mother had made her career. What twelve-year-old wants to tour full-time?

She struck a chord, enjoying the way the sound bounced off the walls.

I'll fly to you, will you fly to me?

The words bounced around her head.

What if she went into producing? She didn't really know her way around a sound board, but she could learn. She'd always felt like she had good instincts for sound, even if her ideas had been shot down at every turn. But would anyone work with a washed up twenty-four-year-old who'd been handled her whole life? More importantly, could she transition quietly? Not if the press had its way. She'd never get a moment's rest once everything blew up in the press. She sighed, heart sinking to her toes. Resolution Ranch might be a haven for her, but time was running out. Sooner than she was ready, she'd have to leave the ranch. And Cash.

Her heart twisted so painfully, she couldn't breathe. Her throat ached at the thought of saying goodbye.

She struck another chord, fingers moving over the fret-board of their own accord, settling into a familiar and comforting pattern. She shut her eyes and opened her mouth.

Oh Shenandoah... I long to hear you...

Her throat felt like she'd swallowed a fish bone. She lightened up.

A-way... you rolling river...

Wobbly and scratchy. Like a baby learning to walk. Her throat hitched.

Oh Shenandoah... I long to hear you...

She blinked back the tears. She would *not* cry. She would not.

A-way... I'm bound away...

Deep sadness filled her.

Across the wide... Missouri...

Her voice might be ruined, but no one could take away the music of her heart. And this was the music of her heart. The touchstone song she'd learned the first time she picked up a guitar. The song she sang for the father she never knew, for the grandmother she missed. For all that she'd lost. She might never sing in front of anyone else again, but here, in the solitude of the barn, her broken, scratchy voice could sing. And the ache she carried inside her might ease.

In spite of her efforts, a tear leaked out as she moved into the second verse. And she let them come. She couldn't sing full voice, it hurt too much. But it was something. And after so many months of enforced silence, it was freeing to just let go.

Across the wide... Missouri...

The last note faded to silence. Her throat felt prickly. A little achy. Heart heavy, she bent and took a gulp of hot tea. No amount of hot tea or vocal rest would give back what she lost. If this is what she felt like after one song, there was no way she could make it through a set, let alone a show.

Her fingers moved over the strings again, this time moving through the changes to her first huge hit. But instead of the upbeat tempo her mother and Franco had insisted she record it at, she took it slow. The way she'd wanted to produce the song. The way she'd performed it the last time she'd sung in front of a crowd. Pain wrapped around her heart like a vice. She didn't like thinking about that night, but the crowd had been stellar. Magic. She'd treasure that for the rest of her life.

Dance with me… under the stars of a moonless sky…

Maybe they'd been right – the song had been an instant hit. But she always felt it lacked something that was there when the tempo was slower. Sweeter. And the audience had agreed. At least that night. She sang the first verse and circled back to the chorus.

"*Ohmygod it's YOU,*" a voice squealed. "I *knew* it. You're *Kaycee Starr.*"

CHAPTER 16

"*WHAT?*" KATE'S HEART slammed into her throat, and she nearly dropped her guitar as her eyes snapped to the woman belonging to the voice. Emma Sinclaire. The woman Travis hired to do publicity for the ranch. And she had a phone. *OhnoOhnoOhnoOhno.* "What are you *doing?*" she screeched, jumping to her feet, pain ripping through her throat. "OhmyGod, you have to erase that right now." She stumbled to the woman, hand extended.

Emma stuffed the phone into her pocket. "I'm right, aren't I? You're Kaycee Starr."

"Give me your phone," she begged hoarsely.

"What are you talking about? You're amazing. I should have recorded that first piece."

Kate's eyes grew wide as her stomach dropped to her toes. "How long have you been here?" There was no use denying who she was, but maybe she could convince Emma to keep quiet.

"Long enough to know you don't need to be communicating with pen and paper." Emma crossed her arms, eyeing her suspiciously. "What's going on?"

"Nothing. I was just taking a break." Kate's mind raced. How was she going to explain herself? Emma could ruin everything.

Emma crossed her arms, scowling. "Why are you here?

You don't need this job." She narrowed her eyes. "Is this some kind of a publicity stunt? I'm not going to let you take advantage of my friends."

Kate's shoulders drooped. "I swear that's not it at all." The last thing she wanted was to take advantage of anyone. She just needed space to figure out her life. And time to recover. "I need this job," she said quietly.

"No, you don't. You have more money than everyone in town combined."

Kate shook her head. "You don't understand. *Please.*" She held out her hand. "Can I please have the phone? I-I-I'll pay you." Anything. She couldn't risk people seeing that video. Especially when her voice was a husk.

"You think everyone can be bought?" Emma's voice rose. "I don't want your money. I want to know why you're here at the ranch taking advantage of my friends."

Kate held up her hands in supplication. "I know it looks bad, but I swear, I'm not."

Emma's mouth flattened. "Start talking."

Kate gestured to the hay bales, heart sinking. PR types were the worst. They only saw dollar signs for their agencies. "Can we sit?"

Emma shrugged. "Sure."

Kate returned to where she'd been sitting and paused to gather her thoughts while she drank more hot tea. It felt like a prickly pear cactus had sprouted in her throat. *Think, Kate. Think.* What would Helene do? She almost laughed at the absurdity of it. But if she was going to take control of her future, she had to be her own advocate. No one could do that for her anymore.

Kate rolled back her shoulders, meeting Emma's mistrustful gaze head-on. "Before I tell you anything, I need to know you're not going to go to the press, or sell my story to the tabloids."

Emma's eyes snapped angrily. "I know show biz is filled with slimebags, but this is Prairie. And if you believe that any one of us here would sell you out, then maybe you should sneak back to your castle in Kentucky—"

"Tennessee."

"I don't care where it is. I thought you were here to help the ranch."

Guilt ate at Kate. "I am. But it's more complicated than that."

Emma crossed her arms. "Try me."

"I'll need you to sign a non-disclosure." Would her mother be proud of her for once? Sticking to her guns like this?

Emma made a face and waved a hand. "I sign them all the time in my line of work." She reached into her bag and pulled out a folder and a pen. She found the form and scrawled her signature. "Here. It's Royal Fountain Media's standard ND." She practically shoved it at her.

Kate scanned the form. It was the standard gobbledygook and would suffice. She folded the form and slipped it into her back pocket. She took a deep breath, pulse thready with anxiety. "How much do you know about me?"

"I heard you canceled a tour and disappeared from the public eye."

Kate studied her carefully. She didn't look like she was holding anything back, but it was hard to tell. "Anything else?"

She shook her head. "I'm sorry. I'm so busy I don't pay attention to much superstar drama."

Kate ignored the barb, even though it hurt. As far as superstars went, she was pretty low-key. And the only drama in her life came from others. "No one knows I'm here. As far as the paparazzi are concerned, I've become a recluse at my estate."

"You mean you never leave?" Emma sounded incredulous.

"Rarely. I make it work. Or I did..." her voice trailed off. She took a drink and continued, heart kicking against her ribs. Could she trust Emma? "I- I... lost my voice. Ruined it, some people say."

"That's why the paper and pen?"

She nodded. "I had vocal surgery. And... and," she sniffed, blinking hard, then shook her head. "It partially worked. But they basically told me I'd never be able to keep the schedule I had before... before."

Emma gasped, covering her mouth.

Great. Just the reaction she didn't want to see. Kate felt sick.

"The doctor said that I should- I should- find a different career." The last part came out in a whisper. The finality of it all crashed down on her. Her career was dead. And giving voice to that reality cut to her soul.

Silence filled the barn.

"But you sounded beautiful," Emma said softly.

Kate laughed bitterly. "I can't even tell. Everything feels so foreign. Broken."

"Well if this is broken Kaycee Starr, I'll take it. And so will a ton of other people, I bet. Question is, what do *you* want to do?"

Kate brushed a hand over her eyes. "I don't know who I am without a guitar in my hands. That's part of why I came here. I grew up around horses. And I figured if I could just make it through a day caring for the animals without breaking down, then maybe that was a start."

"So you came here to start over?"

"I needed a place where the paparazzi would never think to look. And I figured if Resolution Ranch was a place for struggling veterans, maybe it would be okay for me to struggle here, too."

"Has it helped?"

"Being here?" Kate nodded. "Yeah. Everyone's been great. But no one knows who I am. I'm just Kate here." She narrowed her eyes. "And I want it to stay that way. I can go into town, and there are no photographers, no reporters wanting the latest scoop."

Emma stared at her shrewdly. Warning bells sounded in Kate's head. Was Emma going to try and blackmail her?

"I'm planning a concert here for the beginning of May. You should sing at it."

She shook her head vigorously, perilously close to tears. Emma didn't get it. Not remotely. "Are you kidding?" she barked bitterly. "My throat feels like sandpaper. My voice hurts just from singing two songs. I–"

"But what if I could guarantee your privacy and security, would you consider it? Maybe it would help you feel better… singing a little?"

Singing lightly by herself *had* made her feel better. But there was a huge difference between shower singing and giving a concert. "I'm sorry." She shook her head, regret consuming her. "My voice is ruined. I wouldn't last ten minutes onstage."

"I don't believe that. The world needs to hear your voice, Kaycee–"

"*Please*," Kate begged. "I'm Kate. Kaycee… Kaycee's finished."

Emma crossed her arms stubbornly. "I don't believe that for a second. People would be thrilled to hear you. I'm no musical expert, but you sounded amazing just now. And having your name to bring attention to the ranch could mean a huge difference for Travis and Elaine."

Kate grimaced. Travis and Elaine had been fantastic. And she'd do anything to help them. Anything but this. She slowly shook her head. "You don't understand. The ranch would be overrun with paparazzi. Everyone wanting a piece of me. Not to mention the crazed fans." She shuddered. "Travis and Elaine have been so good to me, and I'm so grateful for my job here. But I'm sorry. I just can't."

"Please consider it? The concert is two months away, you might have a whole new voice by then."

If only it were that easy. A tear dripped down Kate's cheek, and she shook her head. "I know you don't understand, but I have to accept that part of my life is over. Please? I need to know you won't give my secret away. I just want a quiet life away from the gossip and the media. Please let me have that?"

Emma's face was a picture of disappointment. "I won't tell. But I think you're making a mistake. You can't hide here forever. What are you going to do when the other veterans arrive? Or when the press comes? Someone else is bound to recognize you."

"I'll stay in my house." It wasn't ideal, but she could manage.

Emma scowled. "So you'll stay trapped here instead of your own home, but you'll take everyone else here hostage to do it? How is that fair to Travis and Elaine, or the veterans they're trying to help?"

Guilt settled in her stomach. Emma was right. She couldn't do that to Travis and Elaine. Not after giving her a chance like they had. "Then just give me a little more time? I'm not ready."

"Kate, the livelihood of the ranch will depend on its visibility. And I don't mean to be insensitive, because I can see how devastated you are. But the veterans coming here have been through the wringer. They've put their bodies and souls on the line in service to their country. They're suffering. *Please* think about how your actions will impact them."

Kate's heart twisted. What about Cash? What would he think of her when this all came to light? Would he feel used? Or worse? She hung her head.

"In some ways, we're all wounded, Kate. Every single one of us. We've all experienced loss. Hardship. I know you've heard Travis talking about how we can let those moments *be* our story, or simply be *a part* of our story."

Kate peeked up at Emma. The woman wasn't much older than she was. And the passion on her face struck an answering chord in Kate. "Ask anyone in town. We've *all* lost something. Or someone. Some of us have come through better than others, but no one goes through life unscathed. We get through it by helping each other."

And who was there to help her? Cheyenne, maybe. Certainly not her mother or Franco. Would Cash? If she trusted him enough to tell him her secret?

Emma sighed, shaking her head. "Maybe you need to think of this differently. Maybe your voice, even *broken*," she made air quotes, "could help someone."

Could it? Doubt ate at her.

Emma stood, brushing her hands on her jeans, giving her a frank stare. "Think about joining the concert. You know where to find me if you change your mind."

CHAPTER 17

S OMETHING WAS WRONG. And Cash had a damned good idea what it was. He swung his hammer, narrowly avoiding his finger, revisiting his interactions with Kate since the first night they'd spent together.

They were in a dance of avoidance, and it was clear he was going to have to be the one to break it. And that scared the shit out of him. He could understand Kate wanting to protect herself. He'd read the stories online. The paparazzi were relentless where she was concerned. But they were both living half-truths, and he wanted more.

Come hell or high water, tonight he was coming clean. About everything. The tiny cabins he and the day crew from town had been working on were nearly complete, and he wanted a fresh start when they moved in. If she bolted, so be it. His heart stuttered at the thought. *She won't want a failure*, the voice of doubt chided. *Someone who can't keep her safe. Someone who washed out.*

Cash shook his head, quelling the voice. He and Kate had a connection that transcended both their histories. He felt it when he lost himself in her beautiful green eyes. Knew it when they kissed. He had to trust that.

His phone buzzed in his pocket. He put a final nail in the door frame, then checked his phone. Travis.

I need you and Kate at the house asap.

A sick feeling developed in the pit of his stomach. Kate would be in the barn, she'd beat him to the house. "Travis needs something at the house. I'll be back," he called to Mike McAllister, one of the guys helping with the build.

He jogged the distance, arriving at the porch sweaty and out of breath. Kate sat on the steps, waiting, eyes wide with fear. Danger warnings prickled at the back of his neck. He held his hand out to Kate. "Don't worry, babe, whatever it is, we'll meet it together."

She nodded, and they stepped into the house. Four pairs of eyes turned their direction. Travis looked fit to be tied. His wife, Elaine, stood uncomfortably by his side. Sterling stood by the mantle, a determined expression on his face. What the fuck? Was this an ambush? Beside him, Kate gasped, body going tense. "What's going on?" he asked more roughly than he should.

Emma Sinclaire, in charge of the ranch's publicity and fundraising efforts shot an apologetic look at Kate, who shook her head, eyes filled with panic. In that second, everything became crystal clear. Emma must have discovered Kate's identity. But how? She hardly had any interaction with Emma. Emma cleared her throat. "Kate. I know I'm betraying your confidence, and I'm so very sorry, but there are some new developments with the ranch that concern you."

"Will someone tell me what the fuck is going on?" Travis bit out.

Goddammit. It wasn't supposed to go this way. In all the scenarios Cash had imagined when it came to letting Kate know he knew who she was, this one hadn't crossed his mind. Which meant he needed to step the fuck up right now or lose his chance. Do or die time. Pulse hammering in his ears, he stepped forward, arms folded across his chest. "I should have told you sooner, Trav, but your ranch hand Kate, is actually Kaycee Starr."

Kate's face went white, and she spun to him. "What? How did you know? No one knows." She glanced across to Emma, mouth pinched with worry. "Well, except Emma."

"I've known since the moment I laid eyes on you."

Her eyes grew wide. "How?" she whispered.

Cash cleared his throat and shot a stern glance over to Travis. "We can discuss that later." Then, he turned to Sterling. Fuck. It was obvious he knew too. What in the hell was going on? Had Emma let the cat out of the bag? His veins turned to ice. If either of them were trying to capitalize on Kate's stardom, he would personally take them out back and knock sense into them. "I want to know what's so important that you've found it necessary to blow her cover," he said tightly.

"Trace McBride," Sterling answered.

"Trace McBride? The actor?" Travis repeated incredulously.

Sterling nodded once. "He's coming to play for Army at the exhibition game next weekend."

Great. The place would be crawling with little cockroaches and their damned cameras.

"I see," answered Travis. "That's great news. But it does present some problems. We need to alert Weston. We'll have to bump up security. Does he have a place to stay?"

"Not yet."

"I'm sure he can stay at the hunting lodge," Emma piped up. "I'll check with Jamey and Brodie."

Travis nodded once, then cocked his head, studying Kate. "I wouldn't have known you from Adam. But having you here does present some issues." He furrowed his brows. "Can I still call you Kate?"

She nodded, looking utterly defeated. "Please. It's my given name."

Cash's heart went out to her. He wanted nothing more than to wrap her in his arms and let her know everything would be okay. That if it was within his power, he'd make it okay. Whatever it took.

Travis looked at the group. "For Kate's sake, and ours, it will be better if the press is camped out on the other side of town."

"But this will impact the activities we're planning at the ranch," Emma pointed out. "What do we do for the poker tournament and the concert in May?" Emma turned to Kate, looking positively mercenary. "I still think Kaycee, *Kate*, should make a surprise appearance. The audience would be thrilled."

Cash didn't like it one bit. How dare she expose Kate, then put her on the spot to do a concert?

Kate's mouth flattened, and she shook her head. "I've already said no. As long as no one knows I'm here, I don't see that activity on the ranch would invade my privacy. But if you're worried..." Her shoulders drooped in defeat. "Maybe it's time for me to go home." She spoke quietly, her despair permeating the room.

"You're welcome to stay as long as you like, Kate," Travis said, softening. "You have a real gift with the horses. I'd hate to lose you."

Kate nodded, and gave him a small smile. The crushed look in her eyes pierced Cash to the core. "I appreciate that. But I can't hide out here forever."

She turned to him, and the rest of the room fell away. Her eyes, her face, contained all the words that hung unspoken between them. He longed to reach for her. "Please don't tell anyone I'm here," she pleaded. "I…" she took a ragged breath, eyes falling to the floor. "It would mean a lot to me to have these final weeks of privacy before I have to, have to… face the music." She smiled weakly at her joke.

Travis answered first. "Of course. We keep this under wraps." His voice brooked no argument, not that any of them would betray her trust. Travis eyed each of them. "Kaycee's part of our ranch family now. We do for her as we'd do for any of us."

Emma dug in her bag. "Kate, if it will make you more comfortable, I have additional copies of Royal Fountain's non-disclosures. They're the same form that I signed for you, and I can modify them for the ranch. We can sign them right now." She looked to Travis for confirmation. He nodded.

"I'd appreciate that," Kate answered after a moment. Then she glanced his direction looking guilty. "I hope you understand."

Cash nodded.

"It's hard to know who to trust," she murmured, face turning pink.

More than anything he wanted to tell her she could trust him. But could she? When she'd put her trust in him once before and he'd failed her? The words turned to dust in his mouth.

Cash was the last to sign, not that it mattered, he'd never betray her secret. He touched her elbow. "I'll walk you back."

Not meeting his eyes, she nodded.

Cash glanced over to Sterling. "Can you see to the day help? I'm going to look after Kate."

Sterling nodded.

Cash held the door for Kate, then followed her off the

porch and across the yard to the path they used to reach their trailers. They walked in silence, his hand at the small of her back. But the turmoil in Cash's head was anything but silent.

It was time to tell her everything.

CHAPTER 18

K ATE DIDN'T SAY a word the entire hike back to their
trailers, but she bristled with questions. Cash could see it
in the way her shoulders pinched, in the tightness around her
mouth.

Gently, he steered her to his trailer. Better to show her
than to simply tell her. As soon as he shut the door behind
them, she turned to him, eyes snapping.

"How did you know? And why didn't you say anything?"

"Your mother is Helene Montgomery. Your agent is
Franco DiAngelo, who is an asshole, by the way. I didn't want
to compromise your safety in case you were in some kind of
witness protection."

Her face paled. "But how did you know?" she whispered.

He regarded her steadily for a moment, then headed for
the bathroom.

"Answer me, Cash," she called after him, trailing behind.

Holding her gaze in the mirror, he pulled off his shirt.
Her eyes flashed hungrily as they tracked down his chest. His
blood began to race. Would she still look at him like that
when this was all over? If he had any say in it, she would.

Opening the medicine cabinet, he reached for his trimmer. "I could ask you the same thing. Why are you here?
Pretending to be someone you're not?"

Her brows scrunched together. "It's not like that. I'm

Kate. For real. I was born Kate Montgomery."

"But the world knows you as Kaycee Starr." He spoke without emotion, slowly trimming his beard back, so only a shadow remained.

Her shoulders slumped, and she leaned against the door jamb, nodding. "Yeah," she whispered.

"Why are you here, Kate?"

Her gaze collided with his in the mirror, emotions flitting through her eyes with the speed of a newsfeed. "I wanted a fresh start. A chance to be me without... without all the garbage."

He'd experienced the three-ringed circus she lived in, but still... to just *disappear?* "But why?"

She glared at him, then her face crumpled. "For starters, I lost my voice." She spoke so softly, he had to strain to hear her over the buzz of the trimmer. "And vocal surgery didn't make it better." Her voice was laced with anguish. "My career is over. And once that news gets out, I'll be ruined. The paparazzi will have a heyday. Vocal damage is like a big scarlet letter. People who beat down my doors to collaborate with me won't even answer the phone. I've been performing since I was twelve. It's all I know."

He itched to take her in his arms.

"Why Prairie?"

She shrugged. "No reason. Cheyenne, the fiddle player in my band, had been here before. Said the people were nice and it was probably the last place the press would look for me."

True.

She continued. "I know it's selfish, but I wanted people to see me for me. Not my fame. Not my voice. Just plain 'ole Kate."

He swept his clippings into the trash, and turned on the

faucet, letting the water pour over his fingers until it ran hot. He rinsed out the sink, and applied a layer of foam to his jaw. "Nothing plain about you, Kate."

He grabbed a razor, tensing his arm to keep his hand from trembling. Last thing he needed was a gash on his face. He pulled the skin on his cheek tight, and pulled the razor down. "You're unforgettable. It doesn't matter what color your hair is, or what your voice sounds like."

He risked a glance at her in the mirror. She stared, transfixed, as bit by bit, the mask he'd hid behind washed down the drain. But there was no recognition on her face, at least not yet. His heart twisted painfully, but he gave himself a mental shake. Why would she remember him? They'd hardly spoken two words to each other. His job as protection wasn't to be noticed, it was to keep her safe, and he'd failed. Better she shouldn't remember him. He rinsed the razor and continued. "Your stalker is Eugene R. Williams, age forty-six. Arrested at Nissan Stadium on August 12th."

"You could have read that in the paper," she hissed, eyes glittering.

"I could have, but I didn't." His left hand started to tremble, and he grabbed a towel, pressing it to his face, heart punching a hole through his ribs. "I was there," he spoke into the towel.

Dropping his hands, he braced himself on the edge of the sink, holding her gaze in the reflection. "Look closely, Kate."

Her face was the picture of concentration as her eyes flicked over his face, taking in the details. She'd figure it out soon enough. He just needed to jog her memory a little more.

He lotioned his face, then spun, leaning on the edge and crossing his arms, staring at her hard. "Look at me," he said roughly, a sudden surge of emotion making his voice thick.

"Do you know who I am? Do you know why I recognized you the second I saw you?" He could hardly hear his voice through the buzzing in his ears.

Her eyes widened as recognition dawned on her face. Heat raced up his spine, his ears burned. He was going to be sick.

She snapped her fingers, as if calling the memory down. "Deuce. It's Deuce, isn't it? You laughed at my glitter."

His lungs felt like a tourniquet had cinched them. He couldn't fucking breathe as he braced for her hatred, for the look of condemnation that would surely break him.

She stared at him with a look of wonder. "You saved my life," she breathed.

He shook his head, the air emptying from his lungs. "No. I nearly cost you yours."

CHAPTER 19

August 12th

KATE HIT THE last chord on the guitar as the lights went dark. The roar from the crowd crashed over her and carried her higher, higher. They'd loved the new material, sung along with her hits at the top of their lungs, cheered her band.

A stagehand took her elbow guiding her along the glow tape that spiked the stage floor until she reached the sides. Offstage, she grinned at Cheyenne, offering a high-five. "Girl, you were on fi-re."

"You too," Cheyenne crowed. "I need earplugs for the crowd."

Someone handed her a bottle of water. She cracked the lid and drained the contents in one long swallow. Excitement hummed through her veins. There was nothing, *nothing* like kicking off a tour in front of the hometown crowd. Except maybe ending it. She made a note to talk to Franco about booking a concert back here at the end of the tour. She grimaced internally. He'd have zero problems with that. The man only cared about the money she made him.

"*MORE, MORE, MORE,*" the crowd screamed in unison.

Pride surged through her as she looked at her band. She'd assembled the best musicians in the business. Any of them was easily talented enough to make a solo career, but they loved making music together. And they loved going on the road. The tour buses were lined up in the back lot behind the stadium, ready to roll out after the VIP party and drive all night long to Kansas City, the next leg on their tour.

"Y'all ready to get back out there?" Kate smiled widely at the group. "Let's do *Only You*, and then finish with *Dance with Me*."

Joey, her drummer, was the first to take the stage. He announced their return by kicking the bass drum to the rhythm of the crowd's claps. As soon as they heard it, another deafening roar went up. Tiger and Brian, her bassist and rhythm guitarist, went next. Then Al, her keyboard player. Cheyenne went next, and as soon as Kate heard the driving rhythm of her bluegrass fiddle, she took the stage, letting the roar of adoration wash over her. She adjusted her guitar and joined in, doubling Cheyenne's melody, then turning and giving it all to the crowd at the turnaround.

Momma thought you were a bad boy, no good for me... but I knew better...

And they were off and running, tearing through a song of teenage love and rebellion with driving force. The kind of music you blared with the windows down on a hot summer evening as you raced down back country roads. Just like they'd filmed in the music video that would drop tomorrow. The kind of music you lost yourself in, letting the words take you to a place full of possibility.

Goosebumps cascaded through her as the last sound faded and the crowd went crazy. She was flying high, nothing could stop her tonight, not even the catch in the back of her throat she'd had for the last few weeks. She switched off her headset and approached the band. "Y'all, I have an idea. I wanna take *Dance with Me* more like a slow blues instead of a fast two-step." She looked at Joey. "Think you can lay down a rhythm?"

He tapped out a rhythm on the edge of the tom.

"Yeah, that's it."

Cheyenne arched a brow. "Your mom and Franco are going to shit their pants. You sure you want to rain down their wrath on opening night?"

Kate was sick of the way they micromanaged her. She was determined to take more artistic control on this tour. Perform the songs the way she'd written them to be heard. "If she's so pissed about it, she can march out on stage and try and stop us."

Joey laughed. "I'd bet a bottle of Michter's US-1 to see that."

"On my count." She turned back to the audience. "Hey there, Nashville. Y'all have a good time tonight?"

Kate counted to three as the decibels went through the roof.

"Aww, you know how much I love you. Thank you so much for helping me kick off our tour. Y'all are the best. I have a special treat for you tonight, you ready?" She cocked her chin over her shoulder, giving Joey the signal, and he laid down the perfect riff. Funky and soulful. She picked it up and fingered her way through the chord changes. Cheyenne came in with a mournful, otherworldly riff, making the violin tell a story of love and loss. Halfway through the changes, the roar from the crowd signaled they'd recognized the song.

When I was a child, not more than six...

Kate let the music fly through her, giving herself completely to the moment, to the crowd. If only she could capture this moment and bottle it. Hold onto it forever. Too soon, it was over, and she was taking her final bow.

Her mother stormed up as soon as she stepped off-stage. "What do you think you were doing out there?"

She glared at her mother. "Making music."

"You know better than to go off message like that."

Something snapped inside her. "This is a concert, momma, not a political campaign. And why not change things up? I didn't hear the audience complaining."

"No. That will happen on social media," Helene said acidly. "You need to give people what they expect."

"I need to be true to myself."

"Not if it costs you your career."

"It won't. I know it won't." She knew better than to take on her mother, but this... *feeling* had been building for months. During all her work on the new album. She'd been chafing at the limits Helene and Franco imposed.

Her mother's mouth tightened, red lips forming a tight circle. "You know I only have your best interests at heart, dear."

She shook her head. "We'll talk when I get off tour, but I'm going to start taking a more active role in everything." Giving her mother a pointed glance, she adjusted her mic and turned back to the stage.

"What do you think you're doing?" Her mother called after her, clearly outraged.

"Giving the audience what they want," she shouted without looking back, coughing at the tickle in her throat that had returned. "Okay, okay, okay, Nashville," she said as she pulled up a stool and sat, strumming and checking the tuning. "I can't stay all night, and neither can you. But I'll give you a few more." She'd be a little hoarse in the morning, but it was worth it to be out there, just her and the audience.

Cheyenne met her offstage after she'd taken her final, final bow. "Way to stand up to the battle-axe," she said.

"She's still my mom, Chey."

"Okay, sorry. But it's nice to see you growing a little backbone."

Kate turned at the tap on her shoulder. One of the suits her mother had ordered up, spoke. Was he Ten? Ace? She couldn't keep them straight. "Ms. Starr, I'm to escort you back to your dressing room."

She waved an arm. "Sure, sure." She leaned into Cheyenne as they walked with the enormous man. "We need to get them some proper clothing. They look like spies."

Cheyenne laughed. "Yeah. Right out of James Bond. Down to the code names and buzz cuts."

"Meet you back here in ten? I just need to pull off the stage makeup."

True to her word, Kate stepped out of her dressing room ten minutes later, stage makeup and sweaty costume removed. She'd changed into a simple white dress, and kept her rhinestone boots and cowboy hat. Her mother had taught her well. The VIP room would expect a bit of glam with their photo-ops. The meet and greet passed in a blur of autograph signing, hand shaking, hugs and photos. Several champagne corks popped. Someone handed her a glass. And then all hell broke loose.

"Kaycee, I told you not to give this concert tonight," a terrible voice said. "Why didn't you listen? All you needed to do was listen."

She spun. Terror froze every cell in her body. Mere feet in front of her stood a man in his thirties or forties. He could have easily been a fan, *a dad*, given his jeans and baseball cap. How many countless fans had she signed autographs for who looked just like this? Her heart stopped at the wild set of his eyes, and the weapon pointed at her. Her feet glued her to the ground. She opened her mouth, yet no sound came out.

The world went into slow-motion and fast forwarded at the same time.

There was a shout. Several. The man swung around, waving the gun. Then a black blur followed by an explosion as the gun released. Screams came from all sides. The next thing she knew, she was on the ground, clutching a broken glass, blood streaming down her arm, a large body next to her.

"Man down, man down," a voice shouted.

"We got 'em."

"Get her out of here."

Everyone spoke at once. Her arm hurt like hell.

Two arms scooped her up. "You're safe. I've got you," a voice spoke into her ear as she was carried away from the chaos. Confused and scared to death, she looked up and into the fiercely determined eyes of Deuce.

CHAPTER 20

KATE STARED AT him, slack-jawed. She was terrible at hiding her feelings. He could track what was going on in her head just by the expression on her face. "You look so different with your beard."

"Like a lumberjack from Maine, eh?" He let his Mainer accent thicken.

"You had a buzz cut, and were so tight laced."

Cash winced. "I'm not so sure that's changed."

Why wasn't she angry? She should be condemning him, not looking at him with soft and curious eyes.

"I can't believe I didn't recognize you."

"I didn't exactly make it easy," he said drily.

Her face twisted and red crept up her neck. She looked... ashamed. What the hell for? He was the one who'd failed her. "If I hadn't been so shallow," her voice lowered.

"You're not shallow," he said gruffly.

She let out a bitter laugh, shaking her head. "Come off it, Cash. I was. I can't tell you the name of my roadies. I was too caught up in dealing with my mother and Franco, or the band. And I resented the intrusion of security, so I ignored them. One of you took a bullet for me, and I never even asked how he was." She winced. "But I don't understand. How could you say you nearly cost me my life?"

This was it. The moment he'd avoided for far too long. A

knot grew in his stomach. What would she think of him when it was all over? When she knew the awful truth of how he'd failed her? "Can we sit?" Tension knotted between his shoulders. He felt naked without the security of his beard. Exposed.

Eyes wide, she stepped aside to let him pass. For an awful second, the same pit-of-his-stomach awareness he'd had the instant before they'd been ambushed, returned. He pulled in a deep breath, failing at quelling the fight or flight response surging through him. Legs propelling him forward, he dropped to the center of the couch, elbows braced on his knees. His breath came in harsh rasps as words jumbled through his mind.

Kate pulled up a chair in front of him and took his hands. "I'm here, Cash. You're not alone." But he would be once he explained himself. The realization slammed into him, stealing his breath. He didn't want to be alone. Not anymore. He gripped her hands like they were a lifeline.

"Can I ask you some questions?"

He dragged his gaze to hers, surprised at the softness there, the concern. "Anything."

"What happened... after? You taped my cut, and then the police were there, and it was a zoo until I was escorted home."

"Not much. I bandaged your cut. The bullet went through Ace's shoulder, and he was good as new a few weeks later. I was put on... permanent administrative leave." The words tasted bitter in his mouth.

"Wait," she said as the words sunk in. "You mean you were fired? I don't understand. You saved me."

He shook his head, shame burning in his chest. "No. I didn't. Ace and Guns saved you. I nearly cost you your life and the lives of my colleagues. The only thing I did right that night was carry you out of the room and provide first aid." He'd gone over the details thousands of times in his head, looking for some small shred of evidence that he hadn't been a coward, that hadn't let down everyone in the room that day. All he could do now was explain himself the best he could. "But if you really want to understand why, there are other things I need to tell you."

Once again, he was back at the edge of the abyss, looking over into darkness he was all too familiar with. Would that feeling ever go away? He was so, so tired of this place. Of living with the constant fear that a noise, a question, a memory would drag him back. He puffed his cheeks, blowing out slowly. Maybe baring his soul would be like excising an infected wound. Once everything was out in the open, maybe then he could banish the demons and move forward.

"Are you sure?" Her voice pulled him back. "You don't need to torture yourself this way."

He nodded slowly, gut pulling tight.

"When I was eleven, my mom took up with an asshole. He would get drunk and rage. One night–" Cash stopped and took a breath, reliving the memory like it was yesterday. "One night, he pulled a gun on my mom. I was there. And I froze. I couldn't move, couldn't speak." He ghosted a smile. "My mom was brave. Stupid, really. She charged him, caught him off guard. The gun went off and shot a hole in her favorite painting but only grazed her arm. She was lucky." He rubbed a hand over the back of his head barely able to focus for the pounding in his veins. "I should have tried to protect her, and I didn't."

"You were a kid," she cried out, squeezing his other hand. "A little boy."

He shrugged. "I recognize that now, but part of me will

always feel like it was something I did, I lacked. I was too scared to move."

"But you were a kid," she whispered, voice catching.

He winced, shaking his head. She didn't understand. He had to make her understand. "But I was a big kid for an eleven-year-old. Almost as tall as my mom at that point. And I just stood there." He shut his eyes, stomach churning.

"And that's why you decided to be a SEAL," she murmured. "Because you wanted to keep people safe."

He nodded and fixated on their hands. Her tiny delicate fingers encased in his giant palms. God, what must she think of him? Some hero.

"Then you survived an ambush, and some of your friends didn't."

He nodded again, still unable to look at her. "And I recognize I was just damned lucky, but I keep wondering *why?* Why me? Especially when I come home and keep fucking everything up? I had no business asking for your assignment, and Bones knew it."

"Bones?"

"Head of the security organization I was with. He knew it. He'd talked to me before. Seen my assessments. But I was convinced I could handle the assignment. I *needed* it. He assigned Ace to keep an eye on me. And Ace, rightly, sprang to action when I froze."

"But I still don't understand what happened? I remember the man talking to me, and the gun, but everything was a blur after that."

It was stupid, the reason he froze. He should have known better, but he'd been too arrogant, convinced he could handle a little security detail. "Someone started popping champagne, and I went numb."

TESSA LAYNE

She clapped her hands over her mouth. "That's what cut me. The champagne glass I was handed."

"Yep. I saw Williams pull the gun, and stood there. I just stood there," his voice thickened and he covered his head, shame spiking through him, pressing on his chest like a weight. "Like a goddamned coward, while they did my job and took a bullet as thanks."

"But you pushed me out of the way, didn't you?" There was a plea in her voice, as if she was looking for something good in him, something noble, from that day.

He lost himself in the memory, drowning in it for the umpteenth time. "It was Ace. And he took the bullet." He forced himself to look her in the eye. To accept whatever judgment she meted out. "I took you to safety. That was it."

She regarded him for a long moment, then cupped his cheek. "Oh, Cash. I'm so sorry."

Her movement took him by surprise. She was supposed to yell, scream, do something besides offer him kindness. He turned from her touch. "I don't want you to be sorry. I'm the one that's sorry. Sorry's not enough. I've failed over and over and *over* again to keep people safe." His voice grew tight. "How can you trust me?"

"I trust you because I'm crazy about you," she hissed fiercely. "I'm falling in love you, Cash." She blinked furiously, tears glimmering unshed as he locked eyes with her. "You are so brave. And you've overcome so much. And you never give up."

"I did after I got fired," he whispered, cheeks burning. "I wanted to die."

She pressed her forehead against his. "But you didn't. And you're facing your fears. Every day. I couldn't be more proud of the man you are."

"Kate. I want to promise you the moon, but I have nothing to offer you." His voice thickened. "What if I freeze again?" He'd like to think he was over it, but he wasn't so foolish as to make a promise he couldn't be sure to keep. Especially to Kate.

"You won't. But if you do, then we'll face it together. You're okay. We're *both* okay."

"How do you know?" His insides rocked like a boat in a gale.

She placed a hand over his heart. His skin electrified under her palm, heart thumping against it. "I know it in here," she murmured. "I feel it."

For a long time, neither of them moved. Cash breathed her in, drawing strength from her steady presence. He couldn't possibly deserve her goodness, but he didn't have the energy or the will to fight it anymore. He surrendered to the feeling growing between them. And when he tipped his chin and gently took her mouth, he poured all the love he had into their connection. He threaded his hands through her hair, letting the silky strands wash over him like a baptism. "Kate," he spoke on a sigh when they parted.

"Make love to me, Cash."

CHAPTER 21

CASH'S EYES WIDENED as the significance of her request sunk in. "Are you sure?"

Her sweet big-hearted warrior. Always so concerned for her. Kate nodded. It was time and she was more than ready. "Make love to me," she said more firmly.

He kissed her again, reverently, as if she were his most precious treasure. Her heart filled to bursting. She caressed his jaw, reveling in the smooth feel against her palm. The difference in him was stark, and not just in feel. If she hadn't witnessed him shedding the beard, she might not have recognized him. The beard had hidden his chiseled jaw and full mouth. Without it, his dark eyes drew her attention. No doubt about it, Cash was one of the best looking men she'd met. She loved the beard, but could get used to this softer, smoother face, too. Heat pooled in her center at the thought of what it would be like when he feasted on her.

"I don't want to hurt you, Kate."

"You won't. And I'll tell you if it's too much."

After all he'd been through, she needed to show him how she felt. That she understood his pain. Her own problems seemed petty by comparison. If Cash could survive death and mayhem, persevere through nightmares and anxiety, she could find a way to deal with her overbearing mother and move on to a new career.

She reached for the top button on her shirt, but his hand covered hers. "Wait."

Worry fluttered in her belly. Was he going to say no? Give her some platitude about how she should save her virginity for someone better? For someone who cared? But he cared for her. She could tell, even if he hadn't said it explicitly. It came out of his pores, the way he was so gentle with her, so considerate, the way he held himself in check while he pleasured her. And she was ready. No matter what happened, she wouldn't regret making love to Cash for one second.

He cleared his throat, a pink cast to his cheeks. "I haven't... I haven't been with someone since... well, it's been almost two years. And I got tested for everything when I went to work for the security agency."

Kate's cheeks heated. "I've been on the pill since my mom caught me kissing Trent Ridley."

Cash nodded, digesting the information. "I have condoms. I'm happy to use one if you want."

She shook her head, cheeks on fire now. "No." Her voice turned to dust. "I... I want to feel you," she whispered.

He rose, bringing her to her feet, and picked her up, carrying her with ease to his bedroom. "I want to do this proper, Kate. I promise I'll make you feel good. We'll go as slow as you want. And if you're not ready, say the word, and we'll stop."

"Cash." She turned his face to her, making sure he was looking right at her when she spoke. "I'm ready." Arching up, she pressed her mouth to his, ending the kiss with a little nip to his lower lip. "I want this. With you. And I want to make you feel good, too." Her chest burned with the admission. Lately, when she wasn't with him, she kept having these... *thoughts*. Wicked thoughts of ways she'd like to touch him.

His eyes lit. "You already make me feel good, sweetheart."

She chewed on her lip, searching for the words. "But… you know… I want to, I want to…" Oh man, she was going to combust.

"Touch me? Oh babe, you can touch me any way you like. I promise you, I'll love it."

She couldn't help smiling. "Yeah?"

He nodded, gently placing her back on her feet. "Yeah. Here." He quickly shucked his boots and jeans kicking them aside so he stood before her in nothing but his boxer briefs. Her eyes zeroed in on the significant bulge in his shorts. "Touch me anywhere you like."

Her eyes snapped to his. The anticipation in his dark eyes mirrored her own. She traced his body hungrily as her gaze dropped back to his enormous cock.

"Like this," Cash cupped himself and brushed his hand upward. "Wanna try?"

Hesitantly, she reached out, tracing the outline of his cock through the fabric. Cash stilled, holding his breath. She pressed harder as she rubbed back and forth, growing more confident with each stroke. "Like this?"

"Yeah," he grunted, muscles tense.

This time she moved her hand lower to cup his balls. As she moved over his cock, he thrust his hips, pressing himself harder into her palm. She brushed her mouth across his pec, tasting him, loving how his chest hair prickled her face. Standing on tiptoe, she gently suckled his neck and flicked her tongue across his collarbone, continuing to rub his cock.

His hand came to rest on her head, fingers lightly massaging her scalp. His encouragement worked like a drug, loosening the last of her inhibition. She slipped her hand inside his briefs and clasped him. He groaned, deep and

A HERO'S HAVEN

guttural in his throat. It acted like fire in her veins, shooting liquid desire straight to her center. His cock was thick and hard. Hot and like velvet under her fingers. God, she could touch him forever and not get enough of it.

She pushed him toward the bed, and he sat on the edge, laying back on his elbows, eyes glazed with lust. Seeing him like this did something to her, tapped into some ancient understanding of what it meant to be a powerful woman. She stepped between his legs, and reached for his waistband, giving a pull. He lifted his hips and helped her remove his shorts. She swallowed, mouth going dry at the sight of him. In a word, he was magnificent. Every muscle defined and sculpted. A broad chest with a smattering of hair that thickened below his navel and pointed her to his cock, erect and swollen. His legs were like logs, muscles corded as he waited patiently for her to finish her perusal.

She dropped to her knees, hands on his thighs, stroking up the insides and stopping at his torso.

"Kate," his voice came out strangled. "You don't have to do this."

"I want to." Oh, Lordy did she want to. She'd been imagining this for days. She took his balls in her hand, gently massaging while she circled his cock with her other hand, stroking up firmly.

Cash dropped his head back with a groan. "You have no idea how incredible that feels, babe."

"Yeah?" His praise sent ripples of anticipation straight to her clit. It surprised her, how touching him turned her on as much as his hands and mouth on her body. She stroked up again, pausing at the top to smear the wetness over his swollen head. Her heart kicked at the realization he was as wet as she was.

Rising, she leaned over him and licked him from root to head. He tasted sharp. Salty. Musky. The scent of his arousal touched off a wild woman inside her. Liquid rushed to her panties as her pussy throbbed. Cash let out another animal sound that had her smiling. So she licked him again, this time encircling the head over and over.

His hand came to her head again, fingers threading through her hair.

She swirled the head of his cock, then opened her mouth and took him in, gently sucking. Cash's breath was coming in harsh rasps, and his legs trembled. "Babe," he gritted. "If you don't want me to come, you gotta stop."

Why would she stop?

She answered by taking him into her mouth again, as much of him as she could, and using her hand to make up the difference. He thrust with a groan, and she matched his rhythm, nerves on fire. Her nipples pulled tight as she moved with him, sucking and licking until his muscles seized and he came with a shout. Jets of hot come hit the back of her throat. She blinked hard, swallowing, unable to keep from grinning as he pulled out.

Cash raised his head, eyes full of wonder.

Worry fluttered through her. "Did I do okay?"

He laughed. A giddy, joyous sound that made her heart swell. "Holy smokes, babe. I don't think I've ever come that hard in my life. You okay?"

"Never better."

She crawled up on the bed with him, and he pressed a kiss to her forehead. "Thank you," he murmured. "That was amazing."

Cash sat. "Be right back."

He rose, and she shamelessly ogled his perfectly shaped ass

as he stepped out of the bedroom. A minute later he returned with two glasses of water, holding one out for her. She accepted it gratefully.

"So we have a problem."

Her eyes jerked up, but there wasn't concern in his eyes, only heat.

"Somehow, you're still fully clothed."

Kate set the glass on the bedside table and brought her hands to her shirt buttons. "I think we can do something about that."

Holding his gaze, she slowly unbuttoned her shirts and let it slip off her shoulders. Reaching an arm behind, she unsnapped her bra and shrugged it off, baring herself to him. The air crackled between them. She snuck a gaze at his cock. There was no denying her effect on him.

"Take off your pants."

With a wicked smile, she worked the zipper and shimmied out of everything. Lying back on the pillows, she tossed her hair and arched a brow. "Better?"

"Much." He tilted his chin, then came to lie beside her, cupping her hip.

He ran his hand lightly over her side, and leaned in to take her mouth. With a sigh, she opened, seeking his tongue and stroking against it, losing herself in the sensation. He brought a hand to her breast, skimming over her already hard nipples. He gave a little pinch, and she gasped at the jolt of electricity that zipped straight to her clit. "Do that again."

A low laugh rumbled in his chest, and he kissed her deeply, gently pinching one nipple, then the other, until she was squirming and clenching her thighs together trying to make more friction where she wanted it. Cash trailed kisses along her jaw, then his tongue blazed a path down her neck until he took one tight peak into his mouth and flicked at it. She bowed into him, urging him to take her deeper. Her pulse raced, but her limbs felt liquid, languid. She could only focus on the ache building between her legs.

Anticipation rocketed through her as he continued to kiss lower, pressing a kiss on her navel and licking a path to her mound, stopping at her curls. "So perfect," he murmured, placing a kiss on her inner thigh, his breath warming her skin. He pressed gently, and she dropped her thighs open, inviting him to touch her.

She quivered as he slid a finger through her slick folds. And then his tongue followed the same path, sending electric shocks spiraling from her center through her limbs with dizzying intensity. It was so different without the beard. He continued to lap at her, brushing her clit until she shook. She clutched at his hair, flexing her hips, grasping for some kind of purchase as he drove her higher and higher. He slipped a finger inside her and paused. "You okay?"

"Yes," she gasped tightly.

"Does it feel good?"

"Oh yes. I want more of your mouth."

He chuckled, slowly pulsing inside her as he resumed the lightest feather touches on her clit. "Do you want to come or do you want to wait?"

"Make me come, Cash." She didn't know what in the heck he was doing with his fingers, but it was launching her into the stratosphere. "It's so good I can't stand it." Her hips took on a rhythm of their own and when he dropped his mouth to her again, she shamelessly pressed into his mouth, begging for release. A moment later, her orgasm ripped through her with blinding intensity, flooding her in white hot light. He continued to pulse into her, mouth working its magic as she floated back to earth. Then he crawled back up to her, taking her in his arms and covering her face with butterfly kisses. "I want to make love to you, Kate."

"I want to feel you inside me," she confessed in a rush, heart swelling at his gentleness, his care for her. She tilted her chin, offering her mouth for a kiss. When his tongue swept across her lip and she joined him, she tasted herself on his tongue, musky and sweet. Desire for him began to build and she wrapped a leg over his hip, pressing against his erection, long and hard. His cock slipped through her folds, touching on all her sensitized nerves and sending delicious ripples of pleasure through her.

Clasping her hip, Cash rolled onto his back. "It might be easier this way." He gripped her hips, positioning her entrance over his cock, teasing through her folds with the head. Then slowly, he helped her sink onto him. "Tell me if it's too much," he gritted, obviously holding back. She loved him for that. Loved that he cared enough to make sure she was okay.

She nodded, hair falling forward. "I'm fine. I want this. Want you."

"It might hurt," he reminded her, concern filling his voice.

Fear flashed through her momentarily as he began to push into her. But he moved so slowly, so gently, that in a second it dissipated. Slowly, he filled her. She gasped at the slight burn, but her body quickly stretched to accommodate his size. And the sensation of him filling her, completing her, overwhelmed her senses chasing away all other thought. He touched the deepest part of her, and as she started to rock against him, she saw stars.

"You okay?" he grunted, hands stroking her back, squeezing her ass.

"God, yes."

He rolled his hips, bringing a whole new round of sensation to her insides. She couldn't even begin to describe what was happening, except that it felt so damned good.

"Yes," she gasped. "Do that again."

He chuckled low. "Like this?" He pumped a little harder this time, again touching the deepest part of her and sending her to the moon.

"I had- I had no idea."

"Me either, sweetheart. Put your hands here." He guided her hands to his shoulders, then continued to stroke her back as he moved slowly within her. Then he lifted his head, capturing her breast in his mouth.

She cried out from the ecstasy of it, senses overloaded. Tingles cascaded down her body. She couldn't focus on anything except the heat building inside of her, the gentle friction that made her want more and more. Dropping her head, she sought his mouth, his tongue, his taste. He groaned and took her mouth with the same gentleness he'd touched the rest of her. As his tongue mated with hers, his hips continued their slow undulations, each sensation entirely new and wonderful.

Emotion welled up inside her chest, the beauty of their coupling moving her nearly to tears. She never wanted this to end. Raising her head, she stared down into his eyes, bringing her hand to his cheek. "I always knew it would be you," she murmured.

"Touch yourself, Kate," Cash whispered, keeping his eyes on hers. "Do what makes you feel good. Tell me how to make you feel good."

"I want slow, wet kisses."

"Baby, I can give you that." He skated his hands up her

back, and pulled her close, mouth seeking hers in a slow, wet, kiss. His hips moved in time with his tongue, and there came a moment where a fire grew within her, and she began to move with him, rocking her hips to a beat as timeless as life itself.

"Yes, that's it, hon," he murmured, squeezing her ass, before bringing his hands to her front, lightly caressing her breasts and moving lower to the point of their joining. His thumb found her clit, needy and swollen, and brushed over it as he pulled away. Not heavy or hard, but light as a feather. Soft as a spring breeze. Helping the fire build inside her.

"I can feel you," he rasped. "You're close, sweetheart. Let go. Don't be afraid to fly."

With a cry, she shattered, breaking into a million shards of light, and still he moved slowly, guiding her deeper, until he went rigid beneath her and followed her into the light with a guttural cry. In that moment, their souls were entwined in a brilliant explosion of stars and color.

She collapsed onto his chest, utterly spent, a happy smile curving her mouth. Cash stroked her back lightly as they came back to earth. Total peace stole over Kate as she drifted on a sea of bliss.

"You're amazing, Kate," Cash murmured, toying with her hair.

"Mmmmm. You too," she answered snuggling deeper into his embrace. Then she lifted her head, staring deep into his brown eyes, soft with contentment. "Can we do that again?"

CHAPTER 22

KATE SAT ON the porch of her little cabin, feet perched on the rail, strumming her guitar, letting the breeze dance across her cheeks. Spring had arrived on the Flint Hills with a joyous burst of sensuality, mirroring the joy that grew in her heart with each day she passed in Cash's bed. The aroma of freshly cut cedar mixed with the scent of warm dirt and wildflowers, sent words tumbling through her head as her fingers flitted across the frets.

You saw me through my brokenness, reached through like sun after rain...

She'd never had a creative streak like this. And it was all due to Cash. There was no other explanation. The deeper she let herself fall for Cash, the faster the words came. Being with him gave her a whole new understanding of lyrics she'd previously penned. And a whole new perspective on what it meant to fall in love.

The whine of a power saw cut through the air. Cash and Sterling worked a stick's throw away, madly constructing another cabin with a day crew. They were halfway to their goal of constructing ten cabins, enough to house the first class of veterans who would be showing up mid-May to work with a fresh crew of mustangs and then make the six-hundred-fifty-mile trek along the Santa Fe trail to Santa Fe.

Her heart clenched at the thought. By the time the trek

rolled around, she'd be gone. She slid a guilty glance over at her cell phone. She owed her mother a call. She'd been putting it off for weeks, clinging to every scrap of enjoyment she could while she thought long and hard about what she wanted next for her life.

What she wanted was Cash. But she didn't see how that could happen. They both knew she couldn't hide out on the ranch forever. It had been hard enough missing out on the charity baseball tournament a week ago. How much worse would it be in three weeks when they opened Resolution Ranch to visitors?

With a sigh, she struck a minor chord. They didn't talk about it, but she and Cash both knew she needed to be gone by May 1st. On the rail, her phone buzzed.

>**Cheyenne:** *Are you ready to stop avoiding your mother???!?*

Kate huffed out a laugh, and typed back.

>**K:** *That bad, huh?*
>**Cheyenne:** *You have no idea.*
>**K:** *I do. Believe me.* She inserted a flat-faced emoji.
>**C:** *Just remember, I'm your best friend.*

Kate laughed at the next entry which was nothing but crying smiley faces.

>**K:** *I was thinking of calling her anyway.*
>**C:** *Subject change. How is Cash?*

This was followed by nothing but googley-eyed emojis. Kate laughed again, feeling the blush creep up her face as she quickly typed back.

> **K:** *I don't kiss and tell :)*
>
> **C:** *I know what that means…*

Kate returned the googley-eyed emojis.

> **K:** *Leaving is going to suck *sob**
>
> **C:** *Who says you have to leave? Why not open a studio in Prairie? Make the artists come to you… like a re-treat*

That was a thought. Kate dropped her head back onto her chair, shutting her eyes and listening to the voices and hammers ringing across the yard. A studio in Prairie. She had enough money she could buy a place, refurbish it even, and develop her own studio. In her mind, she'd been toying with getting into producing, but figured she'd rent time at The Hut, or even RCA Studio B. It had never occurred to her to take it a step further. Although if Reba McEntire could do it, why couldn't she?

> **K:** *I'll think about it.*

Her thumb hovered over her contacts list. Should she call her lawyer first? Or her mom? Best to get the worst over quick. She could always talk to her lawyer another time. She scrolled to her mother's name and pushed the green call icon.

Her mother answered on the first ring. "Kate?" Her mother's voice sounded genuinely worried. But not for long. "Tell me you're through with this immature little stunt."

"Nice to talk to you too, momma," she answered, pushing away the disappointment and trying to keep her voice even.

"Well? What have you to say for yourself? I've been out of

my mind with worry."

Hardly. Kate rolled her eyes. "I've been recovering, momma. Trying to figure out what's next. And I needed to do that away from everyone."

"Your next tour is next." Helene's voice grew terse. "We've delayed the singles' release schedule long enough."

Kate shook her head, irritation simmering. Why hadn't she taken control of things sooner? If she'd taken charge of her career like other young musicians, things wouldn't be so uncomfortable now. "Momma, you don't understand. There won't be another tour. It's over." Her heart squeezed painfully at the admission she'd been avoiding for far too long. But at the same time, a weight lifted off her shoulders.

"Nonsense. You just need a rest. And some voice lessons. I wish you'd let me give you voice lessons. How many times have I told you that belting is bad for the voice? You should have listened to me."

"Momma, it wasn't my technique." She clung to what the doctor had told her. "It was a fluke. Fatigue and illness. I was just, I was just," her voice caught. "I was just unlucky," she finished quietly. She could hear her mother glowering into the phone. "Momma? Are you there?"

"This never would have happened if–"

"I know, I know," she interrupted. "If I'd listened to you and studied classical music. But you were the one who put me on the stage at the Grand Ole Opry."

"That was supposed to be a trial balloon. A chance to give you stage experience. I never expected–" her voice trailed off.

Kate sighed. This always came up when they were at odds with each other. "You never expected me to get offered a recording contract on the spot, I know. Look, Momma. What's done is done. It's over. And I have a new dream. One that I want to pursue for myself. Not for anyone else."

"I don't know why you're telling this to me. You fired me, remember?"

"Momma, please."

"Fine."

Kate could see her mother's expression, frowning into the phone and studying her manicure. In spite of that, she still hoped for her mother's approval. "I've been thinking about going into producing," she said excitedly. "And I want to scout new talent." She hadn't even mentioned this to Cheyenne, but she'd love to mentor up and coming young singers. Help them in all the areas where she'd stumbled.

Silence.

"Momma? Say something." *Please say you're excited, and you think this is a great idea.*

"You don't know the first thing about producing. When have you been on the other side of the microphone? You need to let the professionals do that. If you're going to insist on retiring, you should try and get a spot on one of those singer shows."

Kate cringed. She was done with high profile anything. "You mean like *The Voice?*"

"One of them. I'm sure Franco knows people. I'll see what I can get done. Now, when are you coming home?"

Kate seethed. But not so much at her mother as herself. She'd let her mother take over everything, *again.* But not anymore. "Momma, I have to run, but I'll be in touch. Talk soon." She hung up and threw the phone over the rail into the dirt. She never should have confided in her mother. How many times did it take for her to learn? Her mother would never be emotionally available to her. That realization became all the clearer as she spent time with Cash. He got her. He *listened.* And offered words of encouragement and support at every turn.

Kate returned to strumming, running a scale and letting the music settle her. Her phone rang from the ground. Let it ring. It was probably her mother calling back to lecture her. She continued to noodle around, getting up the courage to hum a little when the phone rang again. She forced her attention to her fingers.

The fourth time the phone rang, she set down her guitar and hopped off the porch, picking up the phone. "This better be good, Chey, because I just got off the phone with Momma, and I–"

"Are you crazy, Kate? Did you even think about the ranch? That video already has half a million views."

"What do you mean?" she said slowly, mind spinning. "What video?"

"You sound good, by the way. Better than I expected. But are you ready for the onslaught? Why didn't you tell me you were doing this?"

"Cheyenne. *STOP.*" Pain stabbed through her throat as she raised her voice. "I don't know what you're talking about."

"Hey Kaycee," a voice Kate didn't recognize called out.

A man rounded the corner of her cabin, camera in hand, chewing on a toothpick.

Kate went cold, dread flooding her. Oh God, she was going to be sick. How had she been tracked down? Worse, who had betrayed her? "Who are you," she asked hoarsely.

"C'mon, sweetheart," he said taking a step closer and raising his camera. "Can't you smile pretty for one pic?"

CHAPTER 23

CASH'S VISION SPOTTED. What in the everloving *fuck* was a guy with a camera doing talking to Kate? More importantly, why did she look terrified? He rushed the guy, taking him down in a tackle that would make a linebacker proud, rolling as he landed, then hopping to his feet, ready to go again.

"What the fuck, man?" the man sputtered, sitting up.

"Don't move, or I'll break your face," Cash ordered.

The man's camera lay at his feet, and he picked it up, searching for the memory card. Popping it out, he pocketed it. He'd destroy it later. Right now, he wanted to get this scumbag as far away from Kate as possible. Dropping the camera, he crushed it with his boot heel, just in case there was additional memory in the device.

"*Hey!* That's a five-thousand-dollar camera. You can't do that."

Cash widened his stance and crossed his arms. "Considering you're trespassing and the sign at the entrance to the ranch says trespassers will be shot, you should be glad I didn't rearrange your face."

"I'm just doing my job," he whined.

"And I'm just doing mine." Cash grabbed the man by his collar and hauled him up. "We're going to take a little walk." He turned to Kate who stood off to the side, wide-eyed.

"Don't move," he growled. "I'll be back."

He turned for the main ranch, pulling the man along. "Who's paying you?" Cash asked as he kept his pace swift, not caring the man was stumbling over his feet.

"N-N-Nashville Examiner."

"And how much were they offering?"

"Twenty-k for a close-up."

Motherfucker. He let off a string of expletives as they crested the rise. How had this guy managed to make it this far into the property with no one noticing? The old familiar guilt pressed against his sternum. Would he never be able to keep the people he loved safe? "You go back to your bosses and any of your friends who might be lurking around, and you tell them to stay the *fuck* away from Resolution Ranch. Any more of your type come crawling around here, we'll shoot first and ask questions later."

Who in the hell had let it out that Kate/Kaycee was here? As far as he knew, there were only a small handful of people who knew that Kate was Kaycee. No way would Travis or Elaine let it slip. They knew how valuable Kate was to the ranch. Sterling? Emma? He chewed on that for a moment as they reached the yard between the barn and the main house. Was this some kind of a publicity stunt? But it could backfire. Not to mention, everyone in the know had signed non-disclosures. What about Kate's friend? Cheyenne? Was this a ploy to flush Kate out? Or was the breach more insidious? Was some crazed fan stalking her again?

His lungs emptied at the thought of someone stalking Kate again. But he couldn't rule it out. And he wouldn't take any chances with her safety. Not this time, not ever. His mind raced as he dragged the man down the half-mile-long drive to the road. First things first, he had to make sure Kate was safe.

He could ask all the questions later.

When they reached the edge of the property, Cash gave a giant heave and hurled the man under the wrought iron arch. "Don't even *think* of coming back. If I see your face within spitting distance of this property, I *will* kill you."

The man's face grew ugly. "You can't do that. I'll have you hauled up on charges."

"Good luck if you're dead, asshole."

He remained under the arch, arms crossed, until the man climbed into his car and drove away. The entire walk back to the main house, he scanned every bush, every rock, looking for anomalies that would indicate another trespasser. The yard was deserted, so he took the porch steps by two, knocked once, then pushed open the door. Travis stood at the kitchen counter, afternoon pot of coffee in hand. "What's up?"

"We have a mole."

Travis's expression instantly became guarded. "How so?"

"I found some cockroach of a photographer harassing Kate, calling her Kaycee and demanding a photo. He's on the payroll of some rag called the Nashville Examiner."

"Goddammit," Travis bit out, face pulling tight. "I was worried something like this might happen. I'll call Weston."

"Do that. Where there's one, there's bound to be more. I know a safe house. Kate and I will be gone in less than twenty."

"The timing couldn't be worse."

"Keep my wages, hire some extra help. I'll be in touch." He spun away before Travis could say more. Not that it mattered. Travis knew what needed to be done as well as he did.

Ten minutes later, he crested the rise overlooking the shallow dip in the landscape where the little cabins were sited.

He paused to count the day laborers. Nothing that raised a red flag there, nor did he see other movement around Kate's place. He could see her pacing her porch, shoulders tight, shaking her head. Taking off at a jog, he hurried back to her. "Grab your things."

She started at the sound of his voice and turned, face filled with fear. "What?"

"You heard me. You have exactly two minutes to grab a change of clothes and meet me back here." He held out his hand. "And give me your phone."

She pulled her hand out of reach. "Why?"

"It might be hacked. We can't risk anything right now."

Her face became fiercely determined. "Cash–"

"*Now,*" he growled. They didn't have time to fuck around. And he be damned if she got hurt again.

Mouth flattening, she handed him the phone. He turned it off and stowed it in his pocket. "Two minutes." Without giving her a chance to answer or object, he turned and stalked to his cabin.

Cash went directly to his closet and pulled out his go-bag. Some habits died hard, including this one. Grabbing his Stetson and a jacket, he was back out the door in less than a minute. If they didn't bug out now, they'd pick up a tail on their way out of town, and that definitely *wasn't* happening. Not on his watch. Heck, they should have been gone ten minutes ago. But when he came in sight of her cabin, she was still standing where he'd left her, hands on her hips. Didn't she understand the urgency? "Kate. Let's go," he hollered as he reached the porch.

She glared at him. "I'm not going anywhere until you tell me what's going on. I'm not going to run anymore, Cash."

"Now is not the time to have this conversation," he gritted.

"I think it's *exactly* the time to have this conversation," she shot back.

"Not when your safety is at risk, and we don't know why the paparazzi suddenly know where you are. I'm not risking something happening to you again, Kate. *Now get your things.*"

She fisted her hands on her hips. "Your growly voice isn't gonna cut it with me, buster. I'm not one of your commandos."

He hid a smirk. She'd be adorably funny if the situation wasn't so serious. "I'm not messing around, Kate." He looked at his watch. "We're leaving in less than two minutes. You can choose to pack a bag or not. Your choice. You can choose to walk next to me, or I will sling you over my shoulder. Your choice."

The look she flung at him was scathing.

Too fucking bad. He stared back, equally determined. "Ninety-seconds, Kate."

With a little growl, she stomped her foot and rushed inside, letting the door slam behind her.

He'd make it up to her later. Once they'd gotten to the bottom of this. But for now, he was sticking to his guns, even if she didn't like it. "Sixty-seconds," he hollered.

With fifteen seconds to spare, Kate stepped outside, still fuming, a bag slung over her shoulder and a guitar in hand.

"What's that?" He motioned to the guitar.

She made a face. "What does it look like?"

"Uh-huh." He shook his head. "A guitar is a dead giveaway."

"I don't care. I'm not going without it."

"Kate…"

Her jaw set stubbornly. "I'm not. My grammy left me

that guitar when she died. It's coming with us."

At least she'd agreed to go without him resorting to carrying her. "Fine. But it stays in the trunk until I say so."

She nodded once, mouth thinning.

He held out his hand. "C'mon. We don't have time to waste." He hustled her over the hill and back to the main house, putting their bags in the back of his SUV. He walked around and held open the passenger door. "Get in."

"Cash?"

"Get in. We can talk when we're on the road."

Shaking her head and muttering under her breath, she accepted his help up. By the time he slid in behind the steering wheel, she'd buckled herself in. The engine roared to life, and he jammed the vehicle into reverse.

"Where are we going?"

No doubt about it, her tone of voice screamed he was in the doghouse. He'd live with the consequences as long as it meant she was protected. "Someplace safe."

CHAPTER 24

OOH, THE NERVE of him. *You can walk, or I'll carry you.* Who did he think he was, going all bodyguard on her that way?

Kate stared out the window, refusing to look over at Cash. Well, he *had* been a bodyguard, the pragmatic part of her pointed out. And he cared about her, so it stood to reason he'd be concerned.

Still...

Kate hated that her old life had come crashing down on her new. *Hated* it. What kind of a fool had she been to think her fame wouldn't catch up with her? That she could have a normal, quiet life away from the public eye? That she wouldn't be ratted out by someone looking to make a fast buck?

She'd created an unrealistic bubble and stupidly pulled others into it. And now she was forced to run out on the people who'd helped her the most. The shame of it roiled her stomach as the scenery flew by in a blur.

The Flint Hills glowed spring green in the afternoon sun. If she squinted, she could almost imagine she was in Ireland, but for the calf-cow pairs that dotted the landscape at intervals. Her mother's voice sounded in her head. *Even bad publicity is good publicity.* She'd ignored plenty of trolls up to this point, so why did this matter so much more? If she wanted a more private life, then what did it matter if the world knew she could no longer sing?

The thought niggled at her uncomfortably.

"Can I have my phone back, now?" she asked quietly after they'd been driving over an hour.

Cash gripped the steering wheel and stared straight ahead, pushing their speed on the empty back roads. "Not until we know for certain it hasn't been hacked."

"You honestly think my phone was hacked?"

Cash glanced over, his expression clearly stating that yes, it was a possibility. "I'm not ruling anything out."

"I doubt it would be. I purchased a new phone in Kansas City, on my way here in January. I needed a break from my mom and Franco," she admitted shamefacedly. Of course, now that Helene had her number, her mother would be back to her overbearing ways in no time.

"And it's been in your possession the whole time?"

"Well, at the ranch."

"Have you downloaded any apps or clicked any strange email links? Like from your bank or credit card company?"

"Umm, no?"

"Just making sure. If there's spyware on your phone, once it's on, someone could track your movements."

"That sounds very James Bond."

"It happens. But it sounds like your phone isn't the culprit." Cash slipped a hand inside his jacket. "Here." He handed her the phone. "Don't tell anyone where you are."

She snorted. "Because the middle of nowhere is somewhere."

"Loose lips sink ships."

"Whatever you say, mate." She saluted him and turned on her phone.

The phone lit up with texts from Cheyenne and her mother.

> **Chey:** HAVE YOU SEEN THIS??!!!??!?!?

> **Helene:** I thought you said you were through sing-ing... What are you playing at?

> **Chey:** PICK UP!!!!! Everything okay???

> **Helene:** Franco is talking to his lawyer. He's through with having his chain yanked. You're obligated to book through him.

What? That made no sense. Not to mention she'd fired him.

> **Chey:** Kate??!!??

She scrolled through the remaining messages stomach lurching with each new text. What in the hell was going on? She scrolled up to the link Cheyenne had sent and clicked it. All the air squeezed out of her lungs as a video popped up on the Nashville Examiner Page with the title *Kaycee Starr discovered hiding in Kansas.* She clapped a hand over her mouth in horror as she recognized herself sitting on a hay bale in the barn on the ranch. The video ended with a voice screeching "*Ohmygod you're Kaycee Starr!*"

Emma Sinclaire.

Kate's stomach pitched. But Emma had promised. She'd signed a nondisclosure. How *could* she? Heat raced up her spine even as her hands turned cold.

"What is it?" Cash asked sharply, shooting her a concerned glance.

"It was Emma," she spoke quietly, cold sinking to her stomach. "Emma sold me out."

"Emma Sinclaire?"

Kate nodded, blinking furiously. "I'm sick. I don't understand."

"How do you know it was her?"

"This video." She waved the phone. "I was on the phone with Cheyenne just before things got crazy and she was going on about a viral video. She must have meant this. It's me singing in the barn. I didn't know Emma was there and she recorded me. She promised to delete the video and signed an ND."

"A non-disclosure doesn't mean shit when twenty grand is on the line."

"I don't understand."

"That's how much the paper was offering for a picture of you. Probably more for video." He sounded as disgusted as she felt.

"Well then, we can see her in court." She scrolled through the contacts she'd transferred from her old phone, and hit the number for her lawyer. It went straight to voicemail, no surprise. She'd never texted him, but this was an emergency.

K: *Brian – I need you to file a breach of contract suit against Emma Sinclaire and Royal Fountain Media, asap. She signed an ND and video she took of me is all over the internet.*

A few minutes later her phone buzzed.

B: *Would this have anything to do with the certified mail I received naming you in a breach of contract suit from Franco DiAngelo?*

Her vision spotted and her hands went numb as the text

sank in. "Noooooo. *NoNoNO*." Kate had never believed in the expression "seeing red" until now, except she was so angry she couldn't even see. She was ready to punch something.

"More bad news?"

"If you call my *former* agent trying to sue me for breach of contract, then yeah." She typed furiously.

> **K:** *Franco is full of shit. I fired him in January. He can kiss my ass."*

Sometimes it paid to have a lawyer on retainer. A lawsuit wouldn't fix her wider problem, but she could recoup whatever funds Emma had sold her video for, and then give the funds to the ranch for the trouble she'd caused. That justice would be enough. Her thoughts turned to Travis and Elaine. "What will this mean for the ranch?"

"Too early to tell. I'm sure Weston will send extra patrols. Don't worry, Travis won't let the paparazzi fuck with anyone."

"I've ruined everything for them," she whispered, chest burning. "Haven't I?"

Cash reached out a reassuring hand, caressing her shoulder. "Nothing we can't deal with sweetheart. Why don't you shut your eyes? We have a long drive ahead of us."

She flipped her wrist up and studied the temporary tattoo she'd reapplied a few days ago. *I Am Brave.*

She didn't feel brave at the moment. She felt like a coward. What would brave Kate do? Face the press. Tell them to fuck off and leave her alone. So what was holding her back from that? The quickest way to a private life would be to go public with her vocal problems. But it would also kill any credibility she had. Wouldn't it? The great Kaycee Starr turning to producing, song-writing, and talent scouting because she couldn't hack it as a singer anymore?

That was the issue. She was only twenty-four. What was she supposed to do for the rest of her life?

"Wanna talk about it?" Cash asked quietly.

"I don't think you're going to like what I have to say."

"We have a long drive to sort it out."

"Why don't we start by you telling me where we're going?"

A frown drew down his mouth. "Chicago. I have an apartment there. Sometimes it's been used as a safe house. No risk of the paparazzi spying on you there."

"Chicago," she stated flatly. "You're taking me to Chicago."

"It's the safest place I know."

"What if I told you I was ready to face the press?"

"I'd say you were crazy. The whole reason you came to Prairie was to get away from them."

"And that was lovely. But let's be honest. I was living in a bubble. And now I've jeopardized the ranch. At the very least, I've interrupted its operations because I was acting selfishly and was too afraid to live my life."

Cash gripped the steering wheel so hard his knuckles went white. "But what if I fail you again? What if something happens?"

"I'm not going to live my life on the run. Or in hiding."

"But I'm afraid for you, babe." His voice rose.

Her heart melted at his words. Her sweet giant of a man, so tender. "You can't keep me in glass, Cash. Locked away like a doll. What kind of a life would that be? For either of us?"

He shook his head, but didn't speak.

"Do you have feelings for me Cash?"

His jaw went tight, the muscle below his ear twitching. "You know I do."

"Do you trust me?"

He nodded curtly.

"Then you have to let me do this my way. It's my life."

He glanced over. The wild-eyed, frightened look she remembered from the night he tackled her had returned. "But I can't let you get hurt," he whispered hoarsely. "Or worse."

She sighed heavily, pain for them both, at their impossible situation, twisting her stomach in knots. "I understand. I really do." She reached out, giving his leg a comforting squeeze. "But I want a partner. Not a protector."

The fight left his shoulders. "But that's all I know how to be."

CHAPTER 25

CASH STOOD CONTEMPLATING the black expanse of Lake Michigan. Far below, the lights of Navy Pier blinked like a beacon. How many nights and days had he stood in this very spot contemplating his life and examining it like a Rubik's Cube? Tonight was no different. Kate was going to go back to Nashville. He could feel it. The pain of it seared through him. And what killed him? Made the ache gunk up his throat so he couldn't swallow? He wouldn't try and stop her.

He couldn't.

She wanted a partner, not a protector. She wanted cowboy Cash, not bodyguard Deuce. He wanted to be both. Needed to be both. He would always be a warrior. He might also be a lover, and a not-half-bad rancher, but he'd never stop trying to protect the people he loved. Including Kate. But if she didn't want that? Then, she didn't want him. And that hurt worse than the knife wound that scarred his side.

The security phone jarred him from his thoughts. "Yes," he barked.

"A Sterling Walker is here? Said to tell you he's been driving all night."

Travis must have sent him. He and Weston were the only ones in Prairie who knew he owned this condo. "Send him up."

Why in the hell would Sterling be here? Unless it was somehow twisted up with Emma? Suspicion got the better of him. Emma had told Sterling about Kaycee first. Had he been the one to sell out Kate in some kind of misguided attempt to help fund the ranch?

The elevator bell rang, and he counted slowly to seven, then whipped open the door. Sure enough, Sterling Walker stood in front of him, hand raised to knock, looking utterly worn out. "If you knew about the video, I swear, I'll break every bone in your body," Cash ground out.

Sterling waved him off. "I know, I know. Can I please come in?"

Cash stepped aside and let Sterling pass, following him into the living room. Sterling walked right up to the glass and gave a low whistle. "Nice digs. This place yours?"

Cash nodded curtly as he joined him at the window. "Bought it when I got out. But it's been used as a safe house before. Hard for people to spy on you from the water when you're this high up." He bent and tossed Sterling a blanket. "You're sleeping on the couch. We'll talk in the morning." Cash spun and paced back to the bedroom leaving him at the window. No way was he waking Kate up at this late hour.

Cash slipped into the darkened room, stopping at the edge of the bed to study Kate as she slept. She lay on her side, hair spilling across the pillow in a silken halo. Even in sleep, her hand fisted defiantly as if to shout to the world she would be meeting it on her terms from here on out. Unease settled in his gut. He'd felt like this before, when he first worked with Samson. Exposed. Vulnerable. He extended a hand over the bed. At least he wasn't shaking.

With a shuddering sigh, he lay down next to her, tucking her into his embrace. Sleep eluded him. If his time with Kate was coming to an end, he didn't want to miss a second. He inhaled her sweet perfume, the essence of her that lingered on the sheets, imprinting her scent into his brain so that he'd never forget it.

Kate stirred as the early morning light stole across the floor. Gazing up at him with sleepy eyes, she smiled softly. "We should talk today."

His heart clutched. He would be utterly lost, utterly alone without her. But he nodded. "I know." He kissed her forehead. "Sterling showed up late last night. After you'd gone to bed."

"Oh?"

He nodded again. "Yeah. I'll go put on coffee." As much as he hated to, he flipped the covers back and dragged himself to standing. How many nights did he have left? Too few. With a heavy heart, he threw on his jeans and padded to the kitchen. A few minutes later, sounds of Kate's guitar wafted down the hall. He'd miss that sound in the mornings. The way the chords soothed him, started off his day with a peaceful beauty.

Cash pushed the start button and braced himself on the counter, waiting for the pot to fill. When the pot was close to done, he pulled out three mugs and began to pour. Sterling moved down the hall, his step quick and light, and Cash handed him a mug as he hesitated in the doorway. "I take it this isn't a social call?"

"Nope."

Cash stalked out of the kitchen, two mugs in hand. "Let's get this over with then." He returned to his favorite spot, and stood staring out the window, bracing for whatever came next. The whitecaps on Lake Michigan sparkled in the early morning sun. Behind him, Kate stopped strumming.

Sterling cleared his throat. "Emma didn't post your video. She'd never do that. Not in a million years. The ranch means too much to her. Her devices got stolen the day of the baseball game. Whoever nabbed them hacked them."

What?!?

Cash spun, giving Sterling a hard look. "Are you fucking with us? If you're fucking with us, I will crush you."

Sterling glared back. "I didn't drive all night because I was fucking with you."

Truth. Cash whipped out his phone. "Those sons of bitches picked the wrong people to fuck with," he growled. He stalked down the long hallway to his office. It was a long shot, but since Kate was a former client, STORM might be willing to help. Hesitating only a moment, he dialed the number he still had for Bones.

"If you're calling for a second chance, the answer is fuck no, and I told you so," a deep voice answered drily.

"Nice to hear your voice, too," Cash retorted. "I learned my lesson, and I'd like to think I've got most of it under control now."

"The answer's still no."

"I am calling about Kaycee Starr."

"Oh?"

Cash heard the thinly disguised interest in the man's voice. "Seems like a video of her was hacked from a woman's phone and put out online. I'm hoping you might help get to the bottom of it." He could hear keys typing in the background. Knowing Bones, he was probably already digging.

"Yeah. We can do some mining. Do some reverse tracing related to the time stamp. I would like nothing more than to stick it to a few careless hackers," Bones promised grimly.

"Thanks, man. I owe you."

"We'll come calling."

Cash hung up and stopped by the kitchen to grab the coffee pot. They all could use a refill. "I've got people working on reverse tracing the IP addresses from the video," he announced when he returned.

Sterling nodded grimly, then turned his attention to Kate. "I have an idea about how to fix everything, and I'm hoping you'll hear me out?"

Kate nodded after a moment.

"First. I have a friend with a friend—"

Cash made a scoffing noise in his throat. How many times had she heard something like that? "Did Kate tell you that her agent is suing her for breach of contract even though she fired him?"

Sterling raised his cup, accepting a refill. "I'm not shitting you, Kate. On my honor. I have a friend who is connected to a shark of a lawyer in Hollywood. Represents movie stars in disputes. If your agent is wrongly suing you—"

"He is," she answered sharply.

"If you feel your agent is wrongly suing you, she'll help you as a favor to my friend."

Kate made a doubtful noise. "I have my own lawyers."

"I understand. But if you decide want another opinion, you can talk to my friend Jason. He'll be returning to the ranch as part of the first program just before the concert, and I can assure you, he's solid. He'd never recommend someone subpar."

She still looked dubious.

"What else," Cash growled.

"In return, I would ask that you drop your suit against Emma. Royal Fountain sacked her because of other videos that were hacked."

Kate chewed on her lip.

"Look." Sterling held up his phone. "Your video went viral. It's had over four million views since it was posted yesterday. And read the comments. People love it. They want more." He took a deep breath. "I know Emma asked you to sing at the concert. Is there any chance you'd reconsider?"

Worry pulled at her face. Cash hated seeing her tied up in knots like this. But he was committed to staying out of her way. Even if he had a few choice words for Sterling.

Sterling held up his hands. "Even just a few songs? As a gift to the donors supporting the ranch. Think of it as a no-pressure opportunity for you to get your feet back under you." He waved the phone. "You already have proof people will love it."

"But the security…" her voice trailed off uncertainly as she cast a fear-filled look his direction.

"I won't let you out of my sight for a second," he growled.

"I can work with Travis and Weston to manage the paparazzi," Sterling offered. "Whatever it takes. I know it would mean a lot to the ranch if you would consider joining the concert. And to Emma too," Sterling added after a pause. "And I'm sure if you give her the chance, Emma would help you with the media. Make a press release, or anything else you want."

The knot in Cash's shoulders tightened. Would she stay? Would she come back to the ranch, even for a little while? Even if it was only a few extra nights, he'd do whatever it took to keep her safe and content.

Kate's gaze settled on him. Even from across the room, she had this way of looking straight into the heart of him. He did his best to keep his face neutral. To not give his position away. If she wanted to do this her way, then by God, he wouldn't interfere.

Kate looked between the two of them, and rolled back her shoulders, suddenly looking determined. "Can you get me a microphone and a laptop?"

Sterling nodded. "Anything."

"I'll do it. I'll sing at the concert."

CHAPTER 26

"ARE YOU SURE about this?" Cash asked from his favorite spot in front of the window as Kate flipped open the laptop that Sterling had delivered. "You don't have to do this."

Kate nodded, making some final tweaks to the digital sound board. Sterling had managed to secure everything on her wish list, and over the past couple of days, she'd familiarized herself with the ins and outs of her portable recording studio. A little thrill of excitement ran through her. "I know. But I want to. I want to try. I've had words humming around my head for days, and I've never been in charge of my own artistic process from start to finish. I want to see what it feels like. And if I suck at it, and the audience ends up hating me, then so be it. At least I'll know."

"They'll never hate you, Kate. I'm sure of it." He spoke sincerely, but at the same time, she got the feeling he was holding himself in check. Not saying whatever it was that he really wanted to say.

Kate hated the way everything between them had become so stilted. That every glance, every touch, was loaded with meaning. He was pulling away. She could feel it, and she didn't know what to do about it. Now more than ever, she needed to face these hurdles and take her lumps like a grown-up.

"You want me to bug out?" Cash asked, still staring out the window. His shoulders knotted with tension.

In the past, she'd always insisted on no guests during a recording session. No one extraneous in the sound booth or in the recording space. But she was by herself now. It was all on her. Cash had heard her humming for weeks now, singing little snippets of lyrics when she felt brave enough to try something. Why not? Maybe she needed to throw caution to the wind. Do everything differently this time.

"You can stay if you like," she hedged, wanting to give him the out if he was looking for one.

He turned and studied her, face inscrutable. "Do you want me to stay?"

Butterflies took flight in her belly as the air between them crackled to life. "Yes," she spoke with certainty. "Yes, I do."

He ghosted a smile and for the quickest of seconds – so fast, she might have been imagining it – heat flared to life in his eyes. Her throat parched with wanting. They were alone… there was nothing to stop them from losing themselves in each other, nothing to stop her from jumping into his arms. Warmth rushed through her, sending licks of desire to her clit. She wanted the feel of him inside her, the fullness, the friction, the release.

As if reading her thoughts, he moved to her, stopping so close the heat radiating off him burned her. His scent overwhelmed her, masculine and earthy. Music swirled in her head as she leaned in and tilted her chin to accept his kiss. His lips moved against hers, probing, and with a sigh she opened to receive his tongue, gently sweeping against hers in a silent dance. The sweetness of it brought tears to her eyes. She would take everything this man had to offer. Even if it was only a kiss. His knuckles brushed along her cheek. "So sweet," he murmured. Too soon, he pulled back. "Do you want some tea?"

She shook her head. "Only water right now." He looked ready to move past her, to retreat to his office, where he'd hidden out the majority of the last few days while she'd played around with the equipment. "You're welcome to hang out on the couch while I record. I don't think it should take too long. I've done enough practicing. If she got clean recordings, she'd be done with the bulk of her work in a few hours. She could spend the rest of the night and tomorrow working on post-production.

Cash's face filled with concern. "Your throat holding up okay?"

She tipped her head, giving a shrug. "I've been singing light. It feels fuzzy, but that may just be how it is from here on out. The nice thing about a setup like this is that I don't have to belt to be heard. The mic will pick up everything."

The old familiar pre-recording buzz of adrenaline filled her veins. Cash sat on the couch, bracing his arms on his knees, watching her curiously. She felt strangely exposed under his scrutiny. Never before had she allowed anyone to see her process. It was a part of herself she kept intensely private, as if allowing someone to observe her took some of her magic. Yet, every time she glanced over her shoulder at him, her pulse kicked up. He followed her movements with pride in his eyes. Appreciation. More importantly, *respect*. He respected her expertise, her artistry. And he'd never really heard her sing. She resisted the urge to crawl into his lap and put off recording for another time. As tempting as the thought was, she couldn't put it off any longer.

Sitting on a stool she'd dragged out from the kitchen, she picked up her guitar, and adjusted the pop filter. Leaning over to a second stool she'd commandeered, she hit the space bar on her laptop, starting the recording. Her blood pumped furiously as she double checked her tuning. She cast a final glance over to Cash. The light in his eyes made her heart trip. She gave him a wink and turned back to the mic, shutting her eyes. Her fingers slid over the chords and rhythms she knew like an old friend. The music washed over her and she gave herself over to the joy of it.

> *When I was a child, no more'n six, Daddy'd come home, twirl mama 'round, give her a kiss...*
> *Then he'd swing me next, give me his hand and toss me high*
> *And Daddy said*
> *Dance with me – under the stars of a moonless sky*
> *Dance with me we'll grow old together, our love will never die...*
> *Dance with me – in the shade of the old oak tree*
> *I'll swing you 'round and carry you home if you'll just Dance with me...*

It didn't matter she'd changed the words in the moment. It was still *her* song. And she was finally recording it the way she liked. The way she'd imagined. As she circled back to the refrain a final time, she changed up the melody, letting her voice go where it willed. She dropped her head back as the last chord died away and counted to three. Then as quietly as she could, she reached over and hit the space bar, stopping the recording. A rush of excitement flooded her, and she grinned over at Cash, who silently returned her smile with two thumbs up.

"We can talk now," she murmured quietly.

"That was damn near perfect," he said, awe filling his

voice. "You're something else, Kate."

Her throat ached as a wave of emotion welled up in her chest. "I'm really glad you're here."

He held her gaze. "Me too."

"The other ones might not be as polished. They're too new."

"I don't believe it."

She laughed a little self-consciously, warming under his intense stare. "Might as well make yourself comfortable, these next songs might take a while."

"I'm not going anywhere."

Her mouth spontaneously curled up. She wasn't sure what she'd been expecting when she'd invited him to stay, but singing in front of him was so *easy*. Like breathing. She took comfort in his quiet support. It wouldn't matter if she made a mistake. Sang a note not quite true, or bent a note wrong on the guitar. There would be no judgment from Cash.

"Would it help if I shut my eyes?" His voice had gone husky.

She couldn't stop smiling at him. "Sure. Whatever you like." She dragged her eyes away and detuned the e-string for the next piece. When she was ready, she hit record, took a breath and let her fingers fly over the strings. The months of practicing the mandolin had made her a better picker, and this song was perfect for her new skills.

Love's a fickle lady.

She don't stick around for long.

Gotta stake your claim, take it while you can.

'Cause when love comes dancing in, you hold on... You hold on...

Will you hold on? Build a house of love, fill it with more?

She won't come knocking twice

I wanna make it last, I wanna hold on, hold on... Will you hold on?

She lost herself in the intricacies of the guitar part, in the way the verses wove a story of a love greater than the mountains, older than time. As the final note died away, she heard Cash's rhythmic, relaxed breathing. Sure enough, his head was thrown back, resting on the back of the couch. In sleep, his face was softer, gentler. Poor man. She could tell he hadn't been sleeping. She retuned, letting the recording continue to run, she could separate the tracks later.

The final songs flowed easily, and she poured her heart and soul into every word, secretly singing every love song to Cash. Whatever the future held for them, she could at least give him this gift. They might not be her cleanest recordings, her voice was huskier, and she no longer had soaring high notes. A stadium concert was permanently out of reach, but a studio album? Not so much. Especially if she recorded the songs in short bursts. Her throat ached. She'd have to spend the next couple of days recovering, but it had felt worse.

Emma's phone number stared up at her from a pad of paper on the coffee table. Guilt niggled at her as she replaced her guitar in its case, and slowly packed up the microphones and cords. The video hadn't been Emma's fault, and if it really had over four-million views, maybe she could turn what felt like a disaster into something good. Reaching for her phone, she shot off a quick text to her lawyer.

K: *Any word from Franco?*

A few minutes later, her phone buzzed.

B: He got the message loud and clear.

K: You're the best! :)

B: That's why you pay me the big bucks :)

And he was worth every penny. He'd gone over her contract with a fine-toothed comb, and sent Franco DiAngelo a stern letter about frivolous lawsuits, and pointing out what clause in her contract allowed her to fire him at will.

I wonder what Helene thought of all that. She could see her mother's face pinched with frustration at the thought. Too bad. It was time for her to run things for herself from here on out.

Taking a deep breath, she dialed Emma's number.

"This is Emma."

Kate could hear the exhaustion in her voice, and her heart went out to the young woman. This whole ordeal had obviously been hard on Emma too. Taking a big breath, she jumped into the conversation before she could chicken out. "Emma, hi. This is Kate Montgomery... Kaycee Starr?"

Emma hesitated before speaking. "Yes?"

"I assume you heard from my lawyer?"

Emma let out a sigh. "Two days ago. Thank you for dropping the suit," she said quietly.

Kate swallowed, tongue in knots and nervous energy fluttering in her chest.

Emma ended the awkward silence. "Kate, I'm so sorry. I never intended–"

"I wanted to let you know that if the offer still stands," Kate rushed before she chickened out. "I-I'd be honored to make an appearance at the fundraiser you're putting together in a few weeks."

"You will?" She sounded incredulous.

"I'm not sure how good it will sound—"

"Oh you'll be incredible," Emma gushed. "People will be thrilled."

"I hope so. I do ask that you keep it under wraps. Let it be a surprise to the audience. That way the ranch won't be overwhelmed."

"Of course, I can work with Travis and Weston on extra security measures as well."

"I had an idea I wanted to run by you."

"Yes?"

It had only just occurred to her while she was recording her final song, but she might as well float it and see what Emma thought. "I just finished recording four songs. I was thinking about releasing them as an EP, and donating all the proceeds to Resolution Ranch. What do you think?"

"Are you kidding?" Emma squeaked. "I think that's a wonderful idea. Tying your name to the ranch will raise its profile immensely. And you have the power to help raise significant revenue for the ranch. Having you partner with us would be a dream come true."

CHAPTER 27

THEY PASSED THE remainder of the day slowly, Kate curled up next to him in one of his sweatshirts, alternately writing in her notebook and perusing the paper he'd grabbed earlier. Cash was content to stay there, letting his mind wander and cat-napping on occasion. Neither of them wanted to address the elephant in the room. He'd put it off as long as possible, because why would he voluntarily rip his still-beating heart from his chest?

As the late afternoon light faded and the living room grew dim, he couldn't torture himself any longer. "When are you leaving?" he asked gruffly.

Kate raised her head, giving him an unfathomable look. Her mouth drew down in a motion that arrowed straight to his soul. She bit on her top lip as her eyes filled with deep sadness. "I thought about tomorrow morning," she whispered, face bleak.

He couldn't begin to describe the pain that shot through him as her words registered. Like he'd lost a limb. Or his best friend. So this is what it meant to be heartsick. He nodded, unable to speak for the lump squeezing his throat shut.

She cupped his face, eyes mournful pools. "Cash, I have to face this head-on. It's time."

The ache was so fierce, his stomach clenched. "I see." He didn't trust himself to say anything more.

Emotions flickered across her face, and when she spoke, there was a little catch in her voice. "What about you?"

"Once you're safely on the plane, I'll head back to the ranch." Though the thought brought him no joy, no peace. He couldn't imagine the ranch without her sunny, sweet presence. "It's my home for the time being. I don't do well on my own," he added after a long moment.

It hurt to make that admission, even after everything they'd shared. But, baby steps. "And," he looked around the room. "Being here without you would hurt too much." It would hurt too, bitterly, at the ranch. But at least Travis and Sterling were there and would help him stay grounded. While he might resent it, they would ensure he didn't hole up and disappear into his head. And someone would need to look after the horses with Kate gone.

He started to speak at the same time she answered with a sympathetic noise while pressing a kiss to his jawline. "Oh, Cash." She pulled back, eyes flicking over him. "You, first."

He spun a lock of her hair around his finger, then slowly unwound it and tucked it behind her ear, fingers brushing along her hairline. The need to memorize every inch of her directing his movements. "I want you to know I'm only a phone call away. I'll come running the second you need. Always." He pressed tender kisses along the path his fingers traced.

Her eyes shimmered with unshed tears. "I know. And I love you for it."

"I feel like my heart is ripping out." Pain stabbed through him, punctuating his words.

"Me too." Her fingers traced a path along his jawline, as if she was memorizing him, too.

"I don't want you to go," he whispered.

"I can't run anymore," she whispered back. "And you wouldn't want me if I did. You know that. We both have to stand on our own two feet so we can stand together."

She was right, and he hated it. Because what if she decided this was just a fling? That he had been nothing more than a pleasant distraction while she pieced her life back together? The searing realization that she could break him, tore through him. Pushing down the fear, he cupped her face, covering her in kisses.

She shifted, angling her body toward his, and opened to him, her tongue tentatively tasting his lower lip.

"Yes," he groaned quietly, opening to her request. She tasted like heaven. Honey and spring days, and endless sunshine. He stroked his hands down her back, needing to touch her, needing to memorize every curve, every hollow. Slipping his hands under the hem of the sweatshirt, he skated his fingers over her satiny skin, pleased to discover she wore no bra.

Kate shifted to her side, inviting him to slide his hand forward. He brushed the swell of her breast, aching at the softness of her skin, the way it tightened under him. He took her fullness in hand, memorizing the weight against his palm, the way her nipple puckered, ready for his touch. He grazed the tight peak, feeling the pulse at her neck spike under his lips. "So beautiful," he murmured.

"Take off your shirt," she muttered, hand fluttering across his chest.

Sitting up, he grabbed a fleece blanket from a basket next to the armrest and stood, laying it out on the floor by the windows. Then he pulled off his shirt and turned to face her, smiling in surprise at what waited for him.

Kate perched in the center of the couch, sweatshirt

clutched in her hands, creamy, perfect globes punctuated with rosy buds begging for his mouth. She dropped his sweatshirt as she stood, and holding his gaze, pushed down her leggings, straightening to stand before him in nothing but a barely-there pair of see-through panties he couldn't wait to rip off. His mouth went dry at the beauty of her.

Her eyes lit hungrily as she closed the distance between them and slipped her fingers inside his waistband, eagerly working at the button and then the zipper. His denims slipped off with a whoosh, and he stepped out of the legs, kicking them away. "I want to know every inch of you," he murmured huskily, overcome by her beauty and her lack of pretense.

"Know me."

"I want to taste every inch of you."

"Taste me."

His cock turned to steel at her comment. He would taste her and so much more.

She placed a hand on his chest. "I'm yours." Her hand slid lower and came to rest on the bulge in his shorts, stroking him through the cotton. "And you're mine, Cash." She gave a gentle squeeze as she caressed his length, pulling a groan from him.

He threaded his fingers through her hair, cupping her neck and drawing her in for a kiss, open-mouthed and possessive. She was his, and he would spend all night showing her in every way he could imagine. Her sweetness threatened to drown him, the way her tongue danced against his, thrusting and teasing. He licked at her, dimly aware of her hands squeezing his biceps. Twisting his fingers through her hair, he tugged, tilting her chin back to expose the pale column of her neck. His cock jerked at the beauty of her, eyes glazed, lips swollen from his kisses. He bent and started at her ear, suckling her skin, tasting her perfume and the faint saltiness of her. At the hollow of her throat, he licked and sucked until she cried out, bowing toward him, pressing her breasts against his chest.

Holding her, he lowered them both to the blanket, inviting her to stretch out beneath him. Bracing on his forearm, he lay on his side, running a palm down her length. Her hip curved perfectly into his palm. With his tongue, he traced a path from the hollow at her throat down between her breasts, bathing the swell until she arched, offering her rigid peaks for his mouth. He took her nipple deep into his mouth, running his tongue over and around as he sucked. Hard. Then gently scraped his teeth against the most sensitive part. Her hand came to his head, pressing his mouth closer. Not wanting to neglect the other, he gently rolled the peak between thumb and forefinger, giving a little tug. Her breath drew in sharply. "More?" he asked into her flushed skin.

"Yes," she hissed.

He switched sides, repeating the same pattern until she clutched at his head, body trembling.

"I want you so much," she whispered, head tossing side to side.

"I'm right here," he answered, kissing his way lower. "You have me." He kissed the softness of her belly below her navel, slowly bringing his tongue closer to the edge of those pretty lace panties. He licked over the lace, giving the hem a little bite. Then he moved lower, pressing an open kiss into her mound, and smiling as she arched her hips up, asking for more. With pleasure, he complied, wetting the lace with his tongue, as her hips rocked rhythmically. The scent of her desire perfumed the air as he caught the barest taste of her through the fabric.

He glanced up and met her eyes, dark and hooded. His baby liked to watch? Fuck, that was hot. His cock was so hard it ached, straining against his shorts. He hooked a finger through her panties at the hip and pulled roughly, the tear acting like a spark on a powder keg. "Up on your elbows if you like to watch, babe," he uttered. "Don't be shy." He pushed away the fabric to feast on the vision before him, golden curls partially obscuring her pussy, swollen and slick with her arousal.

He pressed a kiss to her inner thigh, nipping just hard enough to leave a little mark. Then raising his eyes and capturing her gaze, he leaned in and slowly swiped his tongue up her wet seam. Her taste flowed over his tongue, sweet and sharp, and better than any drug.

Her mouth dropped open and her eyes glassed over.

"Like that, darlin'?"

She nodded with a curve of her mouth. "Again."

Anything for her. He licked again, this time diving deeper, lapping up her honey then drawing his tongue to her clit, gently suckling the bud. He feasted on her taste as she continued to hold him captive with a molten stare. He reached for her hand, twining her fingers with his.

She gripped him fiercely as she cried out, body shaking with her release, but still looking right at him. Yearning arced through him, squeezing his chest tight. No matter what happened between them, he would always remember her like this. Fierce and undone, hair tousled and eyes hot with lust. He continued to lap at her folds as she rode the waves crashing through her, coming to his elbows only when they slowed. He hovered above her, breathing ragged. "Taste yourself. Taste how beautiful you are." He lowered his head, and she met him, curling an arm around his neck to pull him closer, and taking his tongue into her mouth. It didn't matter how deeply they kissed, it wasn't enough to ease the profound ache pressing against his chest.

They broke apart. "I want you inside me, Cash," she panted, diving inside his shorts to take him in hand. She squeezed and stroked until his vision fuzzed. Taking a steadying breath, he yanked down his shorts with her help.

"I will never stop loving you, Kate." He braced himself above her, holding his cock right at her slick entrance. "Even if tonight is the last night we have together. I want you to remember it like this forever. Remember what we have, and that wherever you go in the world, I will never stop loving you." He punctuated each last word with a thrust of his hips, pushing slowly inside her until he was fully encased in her heat.

She let out a shaky sigh. "Oh yes, Cash. Just like this," she cried out as he slowly pumped into her, determined to make their union last as long as possible. "You know how much I want you."

The walls of her channel gripped him tightly. "Tell me," he panted. "Tell me how much."

"Always. No one but you, Cash," her voice trailed off in a moan. "No one makes me feel like you do."

Electricity burned a trail up the back of his legs, drawing his balls tight as she took him higher and higher. How could it feel this good when his heart was breaking? How could she make him lose his mind when he stood at the edge of the abyss?

She undulated beneath him, and he slipped a hand between them, seeking her tight bundle of nerves. He brushed his thumb lightly across her swollen clit as he slowly moved within her, making sure each stroke filled her completely. Her legs gripped his hips more tightly, and she arched her back and came with a cry, tears leaking from her eyes.

It nearly broke him, seeing ecstasy and heartbreak battle for supremacy on her face, and tears pricked his eyelids as he followed her over the edge into oblivion.

CHAPTER 28

K ATE STARED LISTLESSLY out the window as the plane
touched down in a rainy Nashville. Her heart felt as
bleak and gray as the skies. The despair on Cash's face as she'd
turned back one last time at security had cut her to the core.
What was she thinking? Who in their right mind would leave
a man like him? A fresh wave of tears threatened to overwhelm
her.

She puffed out her cheeks, letting out a slow breath. She'd
see him again in three weeks when she returned to Resolution
Ranch for the concert, and after that? She bit the inside of her
cheek, fighting back a sob. Right now the barriers seemed
insurmountable. But she'd made a recording, something that
last fall, she thought would never happen again. So miracles
could happen.

Pulling her baseball cap low, she waited until the last
person exited the plane, before grabbing her small carryon
from underneath her seat and slinging it over her shoulder.
She grabbed her guitar from the first-class closet. Even with
the telltale sign she was a musician, no one had recognized her
in Chicago, and hopefully, with Cheyenne circling in the
pick-up zone, she could get out of the airport without drawing
attention to herself.

Shooting off a quick text to Cheyenne, she nodded her
thanks to the flight attendants and deplaned. Every step she

took away from Cash and toward her old life, felt heavier and heavier, until by the time she reached the pick-up area she felt like she was wading through mud.

Cheyenne flashed her lights and pulled over the curb, flinging open the door. "Welcome home, hon."

"Back, not home," she muttered.

"Come again?" Cheyenne cast her a concerned look.

Kate shook her head. "Not home. It's not home. Maybe it never was." The ache in her heart would only be filled with clean prairie air and wide-open skies.

Cheyenne clucked sympathetically. "I contacted the realtor like you asked."

"Thanks."

"Aww, hon. Wanna talk about it?"

She shook her head, watching the buildings fly by. "Are there still reporters camped out at the gate?"

"Twenty-four-seven."

"How many?"

"Six, maybe eight. Depends on the day."

Damn. It wouldn't matter how long she stayed underground, they would never stop hounding her.

"Okay. Stop at the gate when we get there."

"Are you sure?"

"I'm tired of running, Chey. I'll answer their questions. Maybe then, they'll leave me alone."

"Okay…" Cheyenne drew out the word doubtfully. "I have to warn you though, your mother is going to flip when she gets wind that you're selling the estate."

Anger flashed through Kate. "Why? Because she won't be able to live off me any longer? Because she'll have to buy her own apartment in town? Have her own life? Too damned bad."

"That's the spirit." Cheyenne hit the steering wheel excitedly. "Finally taking the bull by the horns, huh?" When they arrived at the front gate, Cheyenne slowed the car to a stop, and Kate hopped out, approaching the group camped out by her front gate with cameras and recording devices.

"Hi, guys." She waved, laughing to herself at the looks on their faces as they recognized her and hurried over, snapping pictures. "Can I ask you a favor?"

"Depends," one man answered from behind his camera.

"I'll let you get your pictures, I'll answer your questions, and then you'll agree to vacate the premises?"

The gaggle looked at each other uncertainly, no one wanting to make the first move. Finally, a stringer about her age broke ranks and nodded. "Sure. I guess."

Kate gave him the full force of her smile. "Great, thanks. You get to ask the first question."

Her answer acted like a domino and very quickly the rest of the reporters agreed. She stood patiently, smiling while they snapped their pictures. She removed her baseball cap and shook out her hair.

"Take off your sunglasses?"

Ugh. Her eyes were certain to be puffy and red. "You sure? It's allergy season, and I don't look that good."

"Okay, fine," one of them grumbled.

After a minute, the clicks slowed. "Ready for questions?" She turned her attention to the young stringer. He probably sold articles to Buzzfeed or TeenBop or something.

"Why'd you cancel your tour?"

She grit her teeth. This would be over in a blink, and then it would be *over*. She smiled placidly. "Emotional stress from the backstage incident I'm sure you all covered in great detail. And exhaustion. I'm sure you can imagine what kind of toll it takes to have people scrutinizing your every move twenty-four-seven." She didn't care if they took offense at her barb. It was true. "Next question?"

"Why'd you color your hair?"

"Boredom."

"Rumor has it you fired Frank DiAngelo. Is that true?"

She cringed. They didn't waste any time getting to the juicy stuff. "Yep."

"Why?"

She took a breath, biting her tongue. "Artistic differences."

"Really?" one of them asked, clearly not buying it.

"Yes. I wanted to take my career in a different direction." Let her mother and Frank chew on that.

"Are you seeing anyone?"

It was on the tip of her tongue to confess. But that would only rain down more trouble on the ranch. Mentally crossing her fingers and sending up a prayer that Cash didn't see a story online, she lied. "Nope."

"When are you going back on tour?"

Never. "Maybe later this year? I confess, I've enjoyed my hiatus. I've worked nonstop over the last decade. I think I've earned a bit of a rest."

"Any plans for a new album?"

"Not at this time. Are there any more questions?"

When they'd exhausted her with their banal and cliché questions, including her favorite shampoo, she held up a hand. "C'mon, guys. You know you can't ask me things like that. I have endorsement contracts, and it wouldn't be fair to the companies I have relationships with. Thank you for your time, and for giving me some space."

She stayed rooted to the ground as the group dispersed

and drove away. A weight lifted off her shoulders. Cheyenne gave her a high-five when she crawled back into the car. "You handled them perfectly, girl. I'm so proud of you!"

Longing for Cash pulled at her. He'd be proud too. She'd promised herself she wouldn't disturb him, it would be too painful, but she couldn't resist sending him a brief text.

K: *Missing you <3*

Her heart sank when they parked in the circle drive, and he still hadn't texted back. He was probably driving. He'd said he was driving back to Prairie as soon as she was on the plane. Turning off her phone, so she wasn't tempted, she grabbed her bag and hopped out of the car, going cold when she spied her mother waiting at the front door, a frown etched on her face. So she wasn't going to waste any time, huh? Steeling herself, she lifted a hand in greeting. "Nice to see you, momma."

"Is that all you have to say for yourself?" she snapped. "You've tossed everything into chaos, and the best you can come up with is *nice to see you*?"

"Was I supposed to tell you the truth?" she muttered under her breath. Next to her, Cheyenne snickered. "Well, I'm home now, momma, so let's have a talk. Would you like some sweet tea?"

"Heavens no. I want to know why I sent a realtor packing."

Cheyenne sucked in a breath.

Heat flashed through Kate. Keeping her eyes pinned on her mother, she spoke. "Chey, do me a favor, call the realtor back and explain momma was confused."

Cheyenne barked out a quiet laugh. "My pleasure." Her voice was laced with outrage.

"Momma, do you really want to have this discussion when I'm not even inside?"

With a huff, Helene stepped aside and let Kate pass, following her into the great room.

She'd miss this room, the way the floor to ceiling windows drew the outside in. For whatever reason, she'd always drawn strength from the view, and she needed it now more than ever. Turning to her mother, she began. "Momma, we need to talk, would you please have a seat?"

Spine ramrod straight, Helene sank onto an ottoman in front of the large stone fireplace. "Say what you need to say."

"There's not much to say. I'm listing the estate. Today."

Helene's eyes grew wide. "No," she shook her head vehemently. "I forbid it."

"Momma, you can't, and you know that," Kate reminded her gently. "But I will purchase you a condo wherever you like. Nashville, Florida, New York. Wherever you like. But only one."

Helene's face was stone, but her eyes flashed anger and hurt. "Why are you doing this to me?"

Kate nearly felt sorry for her, until she remembered everything she'd learned from her lawyer. It was time to cut her mother off for good. "I could ask you the same, momma. Brian did some digging. You've taken far more of my royalties than you should have. You took advantage of my naiveté to help yourself for far too long. And that stops today."

"This is about your crazy idea that you can produce, isn't it?"

"It's not such a crazy idea, momma. And if it turns out I'm not so good at it, oh well."

"You'll make a fool of yourself, Kaycee." Her eyes glittered.

"Stop calling me that, momma. I've gone back to my given name."

Her mother glared daggers. "I made you into what you are today."

"And I'm grateful, but you've always made it clear what a burden I was. So now I'm setting you free, momma. And I'd like your blessing."

Helene shook her head. "You are making a terrible mistake."

Kate's throat grew tight. Her mother would never accept not being in control of her life. Maybe someday. She hoped. But for now? She'd have to shed her mother along with everything else. The knowledge tore at her. "Momma, don't do this. *Please.* I want you to be happy for me, to be as excited as I am about this next phase of my life."

"How can I be excited when you're throwing everything away? Everything that *I* worked for? Everything I sacrificed?" she croaked.

"*Momma,*" Kate cried, kicking herself for the tears that sprang to her eyes. "I can never sing again. I'm moving on. I *have* to move on."

Her mother stood, looking regal and terrible. "Then you'll have to do it without me."

Kate gasped at the intensity of pain that shot through her. She blinked rapidly, hanging on to her control by a thread. She'd figured confronting her mother would be unpleasant, but not like this. Some secret part of her had continued to hope, even in the face of all the evidence, that her mother could give her the love she'd always craved. That she'd make enough money, win enough awards, that someday her mother would be happy. "Momma, it doesn't have to be this way," she whispered, a tear spilling over her cheek. "Please understand."

Helene's voice was cold as granite. "I wish you the best of luck, darling." She tossed her head and walked out the door.

CHAPTER 29

SWEAT DRIPPED DOWN between Cash's shoulder blades as he worked to hammer shingles into place on the last of the cabins they were building for the first crew of veterans. His shirt stuck to him as the late April sun beat down hard. Next to him, Travis drew up, wiping his forehead. "We'll have thunderstorms tonight. I'd bet money."

Cash pulled off his damp shirt, tucking it into his back pocket. No sense in soaking it through. "Let's get this roof finished then."

They'd had thunderstorms every night he'd been back at the ranch. Without Kate, it had been rough, but he was managing. The first night, he'd helped himself to Travis's couch, thoroughly unnerved by the thunder. But the next morning Travis had suggested he load a meditation app on his phone. Cash couldn't say if it was the app, or just that he was used to the sound, now that they'd had eight days running of spring storms, but he wasn't bracing for the thunder as much.

Too bad the app hadn't done anything to ease the way his lungs felt like they were being ripped from his body when he thought about Kate. When he missed her late at night, when he contemplated a lonely future without her. He could only hope the fierce pain would pass in time, and pray that when she returned for the concert, he could convince her to stay.

Travis popped two nails between his teeth and went back

to hammering shingles. "If I was a wagering man—"

"And you're not."

Travis huffed out a laugh as he hammered. "But if I were. I'd guess you're at loose ends without the charming Kate Montgomery. There something you want to tell me?"

The space between Cash's shoulders grew hot even though he hadn't had his shirt off long enough to sustain a sunburn. He swallowed uncomfortably.

"I miss her." He could admit that much to Travis.

They'd texted a few times, and he'd done his best to give her space, take his lead from her, but it was slowly killing him. Late the other night, he'd buckled and reached for the phone, dying to hear her sweet husky voice. But their hurried conversation hadn't been enough. Not for him, at least.

The sound of a car nearing captured their attention.

"What in the hell?" Travis grumbled, turning to squint into the sun. "Who in the hell is driving a car out here?"

A navy jaguar slowly made its way down from the rise and the driver was doing a piss-poor job of maneuvering between the rocks. "Oh shit," Cash cried out, sliding down the roof. "They'll high center in a heartbeat."

Travis followed him down, gently landing next to him as an older, very stylish woman removed herself from the car. Dressed in wool slacks, with a chiffon scarf covering her head, driving coat, and big round sunglasses, the woman picked her way through the mud and prairie grasses until she stopped a stick's throw away. She looked like she was right out of an episode of Mad Men. "Which one of you is Cash?"

"Ma'am?" Cash stepped forward, offering a hand.

She refused with a brittle smile and obviously giving him a thorough once over. It was clear he was not to her liking. "So you are the young man who has convinced my daughter to sell everything and move west?"

Was this Helene Montgomery?

His interactions with her on assignment had been limited, and all bundled up it was hard to tell... but her voice, the over-articulated way she spoke... This didn't make any sense. Why was she here? "I'm afraid I don't know what you're talking about... Ma'am," he added, because she looked like she expected that level of deference.

"Come, come, Mr. Aiken. Don't play coy with me. I know all about how you seduced my daughter into thinking she can run a record label."

Travis snickered. "I assume you're talking about Kate?"

"Kaycee," she corrected.

That got Cash's hackles up. Her damned name was Kate. "*Kate* picked up some recording equipment, if that's what you mean. But no one here knows anything about a record label."

She scowled, her red lipstick closing to a pucker. "My daughter has it in her head that she can move to the middle of nowhere and turn an abandoned barn into a recording studio."

Was she off her rocker? What the fuck was she talking about? Kate hadn't mentioned anything to him about a recording studio. In spite of his confusion, hope blossomed in his chest. Was there a place for him in whatever plans Kate had hatched?

Travis grinned slowly. "So Kate's going to buy the old Klein place? That's great."

"Kaycee doesn't know what's best for her career," Mrs. Montgomery snapped. "And when she returns for this little concert, I expect you to talk some sense into her." She let her gaze rest on both men. "I'll make it worth your while."

Outrage surged through him, protective instincts kicking

in where Kate was concerned. No wonder she'd wanted some space to be herself. "Mrs. Montgomery, I believe Kate knows exactly what's best for her. And in fact, I think a recording studio and record label are a great idea. And no one will run it better than Kate," Cash bit out. "If you're looking for us to stop her, you've come to the wrong place. Now if you'll excuse us, we have to finish putting on this roof before sundown." Without giving her another glance, he stalked back to the cabin, climbed the ladder and resumed hammering, hope pulsing more strongly in his chest with each strike.

CHAPTER 30

C ASH SCRUBBED A hand across his beard as he paced outside Kate's tent. She'd only been in town a few hours, but he hadn't seen her yet. Between the re-opening of Main Street, which had taken place that morning, and helping Travis and Weston with security preparations, he'd been running since before sunup. Good thing too, because he'd been too busy to torture himself with visions of how a reunion with Kate might go.

Doubt assailed him as he counted his steps, moving in time to the quiet strums of her guitar. He should just barge in there and sweep her into his arms, beg her to stay. But he held himself in check. Tonight was her night, and there would be plenty of time for discussion after.

"Just wish her luck." He stopped pacing and stared at the tent flap, pulse flying like a wild mustang on the run.

"You look like you just swallowed a sweet-gum ball." Sterling clapped him on the shoulder. "You okay?"

Cash nodded. "Yep, just tryin' to time my entrance just right."

Sterling chuckled, glancing at the tent. "I think anytime you enter is the right time." He grew serious. "Don't wait, man. You got something to say to her, say it now. Don't wait."

There was an urgency to Sterling's voice that resonated

with him. A comprehension that they'd both seen things that couldn't be unseen. A look of understanding passed between the two of them. *We don't run,* Travis had said. The only place he was running was right into Kate's arms. He gave Sterling a silent salute and marched to the door, rapping on the flap to announce his presence.

"Kate?" He folded back the flap and peered in. Her back was to him as she bent to put away her guitar. Awareness shot through him at the view of her very fine ass encased in what appeared to be the softest denim.

She rose and whirled with a gasp and he stopped breathing as he feasted on the vision before him. She'd changed her hair back to its natural blonde and it hung in soft waves, framing her face. His mouth turned to sawdust at the beauty of her. The glitz was gone. No sequins, no rhinestones or glitter. Just his sweet Kate, fresh-faced and utterly kissable. She wore a white off-the-shoulder top that made him want to taste the ridge along her neck, lay kisses across her collarbone.

Her eyes roved hungrily over him from top to bottom, returning to hold his gaze. The air between them crackled with energy.

A smile lit her face. "You grew back your beard."

She'd noticed. Warmth flooded him and he raised his eyebrows in acknowledgment. "You like?"

She lifted her eyebrows too, a smile tilting the corner of her mouth. "Yeah. I do."

God, how he'd missed hearing her husky voice.

The silence spun out between them as they stood grinning at each other. Could she hear the way his heart pummeled his ribs? He could hardly focus on what he wanted to say. "I'm meditating now," he blurted, his prepared speech abandoning him.

"Oh?" Her eyes lit with interest. "How's that going?"

"Great, actually. I feel more… settled."

"Great."

This was ridiculous. He ached to touch her, feel her soft skin beneath his fingers. Why was he still rooted to the spot? They both spoke at once.

"Kate–"

"Cash–"

The tension between them snapped, and they moved as one, meeting in the middle of the tent. Cash dove his hands into her silky tresses, gently cupping her head as her arms looped around his neck, their mouths joining in a searing kiss. She opened to the probing of his tongue with a moan, eagerly responding in kind.

This.

This was home. His intensity of his relief, his love – *everything* – threatened to overwhelm him, and he dropped an arm down her back, molding her to him. Kate was everything, meant everything. His life was a shell without her. He poured his entire being into showing her how much. They were both breathless when he lifted his head a moment later.

She giggled quietly. "I'm glad I waited to put my lipstick on," she confessed.

"I would have kissed it right off." He lowered his head again, demonstrating exactly how. When they pulled apart, he brushed his mouth along her cheek, pressing a kiss to her temple, then her forehead. Her scent surrounded him, he couldn't get enough of it. "Is now a good time to talk?" He'd wait if she asked, but everything in him shouted *don't wait*.

Eyes shining, she nodded.

"I've had a lot to think about these few weeks you've been gone. And you're right. I can be overbearing and overprotective. It's because I'm terrified of losing the person I love more than anything."

She opened her mouth, but he stopped her with a finger to her lips. "Let me finish. You were right when you said that's not a partnership. And more than anything, I want to be your partner. I want to be your lover, your supporter, your friend, and when you need one, yes – your protector. And when your mother came to–"

"My *mother* came?" she squeaked, a look of horror coming over her face.

"Yes. To ask us to talk you out of buying some piece of property here?"

Her face reddened, and she dropped her face into her hands. "I'm so embarrassed," she mumbled, shaking her head.

Cash drew her into his embrace. "Don't be. I told her exactly what I thought of her idea."

She bit her lip, eyes filled with worry. "There are things I need to tell you too, and I guess I should have mentioned something sooner..." She let out a sigh as her voice trailed off. "But I wanted to wait until after I survived the concert to tell you."

He tilted her chin, brushing his mouth across hers. As long as he lived, he would never get enough of her sweetness. "Then wait. Tell me later. Tell me whenever you're ready." His stomach turned into a bundle of nerves as he returned to the words that he'd rehearsed over and over for days. "And to continue what I'd started to tell you. If there's even the slightest chance of you wanting a partnership, a lover, a *friend*-" He swallowed down the lump of emotion that lodged in his throat. "I love you Kate, more than anything, *anyone*. Hell, more than my own life. I don't work without you. And if there's a chance for us, I'll wait. For as long as it takes. Let me be your champion."

Her lip trembled and she let out a rough breath, eyes glittering with unshed tears. "Oh, Cash." She stood on tiptoe and pulled him in for a kiss. "I've missed you so much I ache, and I have so much to tell you. But first, will you watch me tonight?"

He could hardly breathe from the hope pounding in his chest. "I'll be watching from backstage."

She shook her head. "No. I want you out front. Please? Watch me?"

For a second, fear for her safety shot through him. But the press hadn't gotten wind of her presence here, and the key players involved had been tight-lipped. Even Dottie who ran the diner, didn't know. And according to Travis and Sterling, she knew everything in town. He shook off the fear and drew his thumb across her pretty pink cheek. "Whatever you want, babe. I can trade places with Travis, you'll have our eyes on you the whole time. I want you to go out there and enjoy yourself."

She gave him the sweetest smile. Filled with excitement, fear, and hope. "I want that too. Promise me you'll meet me back here as soon as it's over?"

He couldn't resist. He had to have another taste of her before he took his leave. He lowered his head, thrilling as she responded, pressing against him as they drank each other in. For as long as he lived, there weren't enough words to describe his feelings for Kate. If she'd let him, he'd happily spend the rest of his life showing her how much he cherished her.

She pulled away with a ragged sigh. "I have to put my lipstick on."

"Are you sure," he growled, taking a final taste of her.

She melted against him, then gave him a push. "Scoot. I

need to focus. Meet me back here after?"

"I'll be right here, I'm not going anywhere." He backed up, unable to take his eyes off her. When he reached the tent flap, he paused. "You've got this, Kate. Don't doubt that for a second."

CHAPTER 31

C HEYENNE BURST INTO the tent. "Was that who I think it was?"

Kate's body flushed. Heated straight up from her toes.

"It was, wasn't it?" Cheyenne crowed. "Well?" She could hardly contain herself. "Did he sweep you off your feet and profess his undying love?"

Kate shook her head, unable to stop the burning in her cheeks. She wouldn't let herself surrender to giddiness just yet, as much as she wanted to dance around her tent and laugh with the joy and abandon of a little kid. Cash loved her. Truly, deeply. In spite of her meddling mother, in spite of the press. Just her. He loved *her*. And she loved him too, without reservation.

Anticipation swirled in her gut. Based on her conversation with Cash, she suspected he would be fully on board with her plans to open a recording studio here in Prairie. But she wished like heck her mother hadn't stepped in the middle of it. "Cash told me that momma came to visit."

Cheyenne's eyes grew round. "How did she know where to go?"

Kate snorted. "She's no dummy. It wouldn't take a rocket scientist to show up and start asking questions. All she had to do was follow the paparazzi trail."

"So what happened?"

"I don't know the full story, but Cash told me she tried to get him on board with convincing me not to sell."

Cheyenne scowled and crossed her arms. "I hope he told her she was barking up the wrong tree."

"Sounds like he did."

"Good." Cheyenne shook her head. "The nerve of her."

"Right? She'll learn one way or another."

Cheyenne gave her a hug. "I'm sorry, hon. She'll come to terms with everything someday. You know I'm in your corner, no matter what."

Kate hugged her back, the ache in her heart her mother had caused, still fresh. It would be a long time before Helene Montgomery came to terms with everything, but Kate wouldn't give up. "Have I ever told you how grateful I am for your friendship? For bringing me here and for always being willing to tell it like it is?"

Cheyenne's eyes twinkled. "Are you sure it's not just because of a handsome veteran?"

"Oh hush, you." She pushed Cheyenne away. "Just take your thanks. And I expect you to be a regular presence out here when I get myself sorted. I can't imagine not working with you anymore."

"Count on it. I love making music with you, girlfriend."

A knock on the tent flap interrupted them. Emma Sinclaire stuck in her head. "You ready, Kate? If you are, I'm ready to announce you."

Kate shot a grin to the young woman. "Ready as I'll ever be."

"Okay, grab your guitar and come with me."

Kate reached for Cheyenne's hand and gave it a squeeze, butterflies suddenly rocketing through her body.

Cheyenne squeezed back. "You got this, girl. Just go out

give them your heart like you always do. They're gonna ove the new you."

"I hope so."

"I know so."

Kate pulled her guitar out of the case. This time, for the first time ever, she'd decided to use the '57 Martin onstage. She'd only ever used it for herself. It was too special to share with the masses. But now? With a different voice and a different sound? It felt right. A return to her roots of making music for the pure pleasure of it. For the joy of hearing a chord echo and a voice match it.

She pulled back the flap of the tent and joined Emma in the warm night air – a perfect spring night for a concert. Too early for bugs, the air moved soft and sweet with the scent of fresh grass and wild violets. Emma stepped onstage, but Kate was too distracted to pay attention. All she could think about was Cash. He'd laid his cards on the table, it was time to lay down hers. Adrenaline pumped through her when Emma announced her name, but she didn't hear the applause or shouts of excitement from the crowd. She kept going over the new lyrics in her head.

Cheyenne gave her a little push from behind, and in a fog, she hopped up the stairs and stepped into the lights. It was a small stage, nothing fancy. But she didn't need fancy, or fireworks and smoke machines. All she needed was her guitar, a stool and a couple of microphones. As soon as she settled herself, she scanned the crowd, squinting through the lights until she found Cash standing on the far right, a few rows back. Giving him a smile, she strummed her guitar, and the audience fell silent, their expectation palpable.

For one brief second, panic flooded her, and she was overcome with the urge to run offstage. But then it passed, and she was just a woman with a guitar, sharing a few songs. Much like she did the first time she set foot on the Opry stage a dozen years ago. She gave a second strum and leaned into the mic.

"Hi y'all."

She was bombarded with a chorus of hello's, hi's, and how are you's.

"Aww, I haven't even sung yet. Are ya sure you're ready?"

More shouts from the audience.

"Well, if you've listened to my EP that I released to help my friends here at Resolution Ranch, then you might have heard this." She launched into the chord changes of *Dance With Me*, pulse settling as Cheyenne joined with a soulful fiddle. She lost herself in the sweet slow rhythm, heart soaring with the words. And even though the tempo was slower, more sultry, the audience sang along, making music with her in a communion of souls.

When the last chord died, the audience sprang to their feet. Kate ducked her head. "Aww y'all are so sweet. Thank you so much. And thanks so much to the kind folks of Prairie who've been so good to me. More importantly, thank you for turning out in such big numbers tonight to support the mission of Resolution Ranch."

She searched out Cash, then scanned left until she recognized Sterling on the other side. True to their word, they weren't leaving anything to chance. "I've had the honor of working here for the last four months, and I can tell you – this is such a special place. Resolution Ranch embodies the true meaning of family, where people care for each other, no matter what." Her voice cracked as she spoke, but she didn't care. She was too filled with gratitude to worry about her delivery. She wanted to convey how deeply she felt about the re. "Here at the ranch, you're given the tools and the o heal. And most importantly…" She turned to where ι stood, and waited until she held his gaze. "You're owered with unconditional love and acceptance."

Even though he was twenty feet away, or more, his expression pulled at her like a tractor beam. Awareness zinged through her, lighting her nerve endings. It didn't matter that she had three more songs to sing, including his special one, she wanted to hop off stage and jump into his arms.

Dragging her eyes from his, she smiled across the audience. "Your support for this organization will allow more veterans to find healing and new life. Even new careers. So cheers to you," she raised her guitar as the applause moved through the audience.

The next two numbers passed quickly.

Before the applause died, she bent and took a long sip of water, trying to calm the butterflies that rocketed through her belly for the umpteenth time. Hands shaking, she took a moment to retune and gather her courage, but even that did nothing to calm her nerves. Behind her, Cheyenne hissed. "You can do it, girl. Tell him how you feel."

Taking a deep breath, Kate leaned into the mic. "How many of you have found *The One*?"

The audience responded with a smattering of applause and whistles.

"Really? That's it?"

The applause and whistles grew louder.

She laughed, shaking her head. "What about the rest of you? You know, the one person who's it. Who you know if you don't risk everything for, you'll regret it until your dying day?"

A few more claps and whistles.

"Y'all." She leaned into the mic. "I think you need some help." She waited for the laugh, and sure enough, it rippled through the crowd.

"So I wrote this new song last week." She strummed a new chord, drawing strength from the sound. "And I want to say to all of you – don't hesitate a second. Even when it seems crazy. If he's the one, or she's the one. Don't let a second pass. Take a chance."

She let herself look for Cash, butterflies morphing into a herd of antelope springing through her stomach. His eyes were glued to her. He had to know she was talking about him, right?

She took a deep breath, strumming another chord. "One more thing, y'all. There've been a lot of rumors circulating about me over the last month or so. Most of them are probably true." Her voice quavered as the words sat in the back of her mouth. Her heart clenched at the finality of it all, and she could have sworn she heard an imaginary door slam shut. Doubt gnawed at her as a future she'd accepted as set in stone, dimmed and disappeared. She cleared her throat. "This will be my last public performance," she said quietly.

A gasp went through the audience. She snuck another look at Cash. His gaze was steady. Strong. And the door to a new future cracked open, its light peeking through like a ray of sunshine. "I don't know that I'll ever stop singing. But I hurt myself, and my voice can't take much more than a few songs at a time now. So this last song... I wrote it for a very special person. Someone I love with all my heart."

She strummed through the opening chords, letting Cheyenne improvise a counter melody until her hands stopped shaking and the lump of tears in her throat dissipated. Taking her time, gazing out at the rapt faces of her captive audience,

.t up a silent prayer of gratitude, for her life, for her
.r, for her friends. And then she found Cash and sang.

On a cold and starry night, love came a callin'…

She began to weave a story of love and loss, letting the
fiddle express what her voice couldn't. A bittersweet play
between heartbreak and redemption. Of hope and possibility.

When storms rolled in and the dark night came,
you took my hand and you wore my pain.
I will shelter you. Will you shelter me?

And I fly to you – across mountains and valleys,
I will fly to you, soaring on the light of your love.

Stay with me will you be my love?
I will follow you, will you walk with me?
Hand in hand we can build a home laying bricks of love,
     make a family.

And I'll fly to you – recklessly with abandon,
and I'll fly to you, offering my love.

Make love with me where the wind blows free
and there's nothing to break the light of the sun.
Stand with me in the wind and the rain, on rock and soil in
     love and pain.

I'll fly to you, will you fly with me?

As the last note drifted away, before the audience began to
clap and before she lost her nerve, she spoke. "Cash Aiken,
what do you say?"

In two bounds, he'd joined her onstage, gently setting her guitar on its stand before pulling her into his arms and giving her a toe-curling kiss, which she returned with enthusiasm, tongue sweeping against his as she accepted his answer.

When they parted, he leaned in, kissing her temple as the cheers from the crowd washed over them. "Yes. Abosfuckinglutely yes."

CHAPTER 32

Three months later

THE SOUNDS OF Kate's guitar drifted through the open window. Humming along, Cash rolled the final coat of paint on the wall behind the stone fireplace anchoring the front room of the old Klein place.

It had been a wreck the day he'd carried Kate over the threshold, but he'd never been happier. Kate had brought in a crew to help her with renovations while he'd been off leading Resolution Ranch's inaugural crew of veterans on the same trek he'd made the previous January. But as soon as he'd returned, he'd shooed them away, insisting on finishing the final work himself.

This was his home, and he wanted to leave his mark on the walls.

"You almost done in there, hon?" Kate called through the screen. "I've been coolin' my heels all afternoon."

"Just a few more minutes. I finished the kitchen earlier."

"I don't know why you wouldn't let me hire the crew to finish it."

Exasperated, he returned the roller to the paint tray. "Dammit, woman. A man's gotta leave his mark on his own house." Technically, he already had. Before he'd left for the trek, he'd spent his evenings at the farm building a fire pit and a large stone patio between the farm house and the cottage out

back that housed Kate's recording studio. But this room w.
special, the heartbeat of the house. And he wanted to paint it.

"But I've almost finished the lemonade," she wheedled.

He picked up the roller, going over a spot he'd missed.
"Fifteen more minutes, play me another song."

"Fine."

He grinned at the pout in her voice. "Patience, grasshopper. I promise you'll love it when you see it."

"Will you at least give me a hint?"

"Nope."

"Oh alright, you big meanie," she said with a laugh. "I'm
going to work on somethin' that's been jarring around in my
head." A second later, she started plucking a melody he didn't
recognize, humming intermittently as she paused, slowly
stringing fragments of melody into a line.

He would never tire of hearing her noodle around on her
guitar, of listening to Kate bring a song to life. It was magic.
Part alchemy, part craft, and one-hundred-percent awe-
inspiring. He hurried through his final touch-ups, then
washed the roller in the utility sink he'd installed in a
mudroom right off the back door.

At the front door, he paused in the doorway, captivated
by the picture before him. Kate sat, feet propped on the porch
rail, sundress pooling at her thighs, guitar across her lap,
lemonade on the floor beside her. The late afternoon sun
made her hair glow like an angel. His angel. Slipping out the
door, he crossed to her, and moved her hair, exposing the
creamy column of her neck. He bent, laying a kiss on the
sensitive spot where her neck met her collarbone. "Sounds as
lovely as you."

She glanced sideways, her mouth curling up. "You finally
ready to let me into the house?"

nmm." He breathed in her fresh, sweet scent, ss settling low in his belly. "In a minute." He nipped kissed his way across her collarbone to her exposed ulder, enjoying the goosebumps that rose on her skin. An nage of all the ways they could break in the front room rose in his mind.

She pulled away, but only to return her guitar to its case. Then she stood and stepped into his embrace, tilting her face for a kiss. He'd never say no to a taste of her sweetness. Dipping his head, he brushed his mouth back and forth across her plump lips, savoring until he couldn't stand it anymore. She made a noise in the back of her throat that went straight to his cock. Flicking his tongue across her lower lip, he swept in for a taste when she opened her mouth with a sigh. Sugar and mint. And lemons. Fucking heaven. He palmed her ass, pulling up on her dress. "Let's get inside before I bend you over the rail and have my way with you."

She laughed, eyes lighting hungrily. "Even though some-one might see us?"

"We're a half-mile from the road darlin'. We'd see them long before they saw us."

She raised her eyebrows eagerly. "Oh?"

Her expression had his cock jerking at the vision of her bare-assed and bent over the rail. "You like that idea, huh?" Giving her ass a squeeze, he kissed her again. "We'll save it for another time. I want to show you inside. Shut your eyes."

Kate shut her eyes, and pressed her lips together, unable to stop her grin from growing. Taking her by the hand, he led her into the middle of the room then came to stand behind her, arms wrapping around her middle. "Open your eyes," he murmured into her ear.

His hard work was rewarded with a gasp of pure delight.

"Oh, I *love* it. It's the perfect color. The color of prairie grass at dawn."

"It reminded me of your eyes."

"Aww." She melted into him, laying her head back on his shoulder. "I love you, Cash. And I love this room."

"How do we decorate it?"

"With a big fluffy sofa right in front of the fireplace for cold winter nights. And a Christmas tree in the corner."

He could see it. "And a stand for your guitar in the other corner. How's that sound?"

"Perfect."

He heard the smile in her voice and tightened his embrace around her, kissing her temple, pulse kicking up a notch. "What else can you imagine?"

"A big farm table for Sunday dinners."

"Who's at the table?"

"You, me. Sterling & Emma. Travis and Elaine and their kids."

"Sounds pretty nice."

"Yeah," her voice trailed off.

Heart thumping irregularly, Cash turned her and kissed her forehead, her nose. "Any other kids at the table?"

She cocked her head, looking at him quizzically. "I don't follow. We don't know any other kids."

Could she hear how loudly his heart was pounding? The way it stuttered when she looked directly into his eyes? He gulped, pushing down a wave of fear. "What about our kids?" His voice grew thick, husky. "Could you see our family around the table? Alongside our friends?"

She cocked her head the other direction, a half-smile tugging at the corner of her mouth. "What are you saying?"

He jammed a hand in his pocket and pulled out the ring

.chased in Santa Fe and had been carrying around ever

"I'm not as poetic as you are, but I want to spend the

of my life doing all those things you wrote in the song.

√e've built this house with love, and now I want to fill the inside of it with just as much love. I want to make a family with you and fill this house with the sounds of our children. What do you say? Will you marry me, Kate?"

With shining eyes, she let him slip the ring on her finger. "The ring is beautiful. And yes. I'll marry you, and I'll be your bride." She sang the last few words, her husky voice filling the space.

"We'll walk through life, side by side." He sang back, letting his voice blend with hers.

"You sure you don't want to go into songwriting?" she teased.

Laying a kiss on her sweet, sweet mouth, he answered. "Only if it's with you."

THE BEGINNING OF HAPPILY EVER AFTER

Did you like this book? Please leave a review! Independent authors rely on reviews and word of mouth. If you enjoyed this book, please spread the word!

Want more? Sign up for my newsletter to get notifications about A Hero's Home, the next story in the Heroes of Resolution Ranch coming in June 2018
http://tessalayne.com/newsletter

And while you're waiting….

Will this Bad-Boy Cowboy reform his wild ways for the woman who keeps him away at night? Another racy ride in the Cowboys of the Flint Hills Series

COMING APRIL 24 2018 – PRAIRIE DEVIL

He's the Devil she shouldn't want

Thrown out of the house when he was seventeen, bad boy Colton Kincaid left Prairie in the rear-view mirror and never looked back. Determined to make something of himself, he scrapped his way to superstardom at the top of the rodeo circuit, leaving behind a string of broken hearts. He's perfectly happy with his no-strings-attached life until a chance encounter with hometown good girl Lydia Grace leaves him questioning everything and wanting a shot at redemption

She's the Angel he can never have

All Lydia Grace needs is one break. After having her concepts stolen by a famous shoe designer, she returns home to Prairie to start a boot company on her own. But when her break comes in the all too sexy form of Colton Kincaid, she wonders if she's gotten more than she's bargained for.

be careful what you wish for

her boot company off the ground, Lydia makes Colton
fer too good to refuse, but he ups the ante. Will the
gain she strikes bring her everything she's dreamed of and
more, or did she just make a deal with the devil?

WHERE IT ALL BEGAN:
THE COWBOYS OF THE FLINT HILLS SERIES

Sizzling, Standalone Stories with HEAs, Sassy Heroines, and
Cowboys you want to Cuddle

PRAIRIE HEAT – Blake Sinclaire & Maddie Hansen
(on sale now!)
PRAIRIE PASSION – Brodie Sinclaire & Jamey O'Neill
(on sale now!)
PRAIRIE DESIRE – Ben Sinclaire & Hope Hansen
(on sale now!)
PRAIRIE STORM – Axel Hansen & Haley Cooper
(on sale now!)
PRAIRIE FIRE – Parker Hansen & Cassidy Grace
(on sale now!)
PRAIRIE DEVIL – Colton Kincaid & Lydia Grace
(coming April 24th 2018)
PRAIRIE FEVER – Gunnar Hansen & Suzannah Winslow
(coming in 2018)
PRAIRIE BLISS – Jarrod O'Neill & Lexi Grace
PRAIRIE REDEMPTION – Cody Hansen & Carolina Grace

Help a Hero – Read a Cowboy

KISS ME COWBOY – A Box Set for Veterans

Six Western Romance authors have joined up to support their favorite charity – Heroes & Horses – and offer you this sexy box set with Six Full Length Cowboy Novels, filled with steamy kisses and HEA's. Grab your copy and help an American Hero today!

Subscribe to my Newsletter for updates and release information for Prairie Storm and the rest of the Cowboys of the Flint Hills Series.

http://tessalayne.com/newsletter

Join my reader group on Facebook – The Prairie Posse this is where I post my sneak peeks, offer giveaways, and share hot cowboy pics!

facebook.com/groups/1390521967655100

Acknowledgements

To my neighbors Todd and Blair, thank you for bravely sharing your experiences with PTSD with me. Your willingness to be painfully honest not only with the burdens you carry, but how you've managed to cope and move forward, helped Cash come to life. I am in awe of you and profoundly grateful to call you friend and neighbor.

To the incredible folks at Heroes & Horses, your work inspires me and pushes me forward every day.

My heartfelt gratitude to Genevieve Turner, Kimberley Troutte and Kara, thank you for both your encouragement and your passionate commitment to telling good stories. My books are so much better because of you.

To my fabulous designer, Amanda Kelsey, I think I looked at this cover at least once an hour when I was writing. You've brought Cash to life for me.

To my assistant, Erin, I couldn't function without your help. Thank you for doing all the things so I can write all the words! ☺

To Mr. Cowboy, Teenager and Tiny, I love you all so much.

Lastly, to my wonderful Prairie Posse. You are a bright spot in my day. Keep building an amazing, welcoming, FUN community!